Forged in Deceit

Steven Wills

And dedicated to Susan – my editor, my partner, my wife - without whose encouragement, both loving and forceful, I would still be somewhere in Chapter 3.

BookLocker
Trenton, Georgia

Chapter 1

Martik would never get used to the back-breaking ride down Thames Street in the Fells Point section of Baltimore. The combination of uneven paving stones and a police car with shitty struts rattled his frame. He scanned the sidewalks for the human leftovers of a typical Saturday night, but saw only joggers and dog-walkers in the dim 5:00 a.m. light.

Normal stuff.

But he didn't like what he saw ahead.

Curious onlookers had already formed at the Ann Street dock. Martik noted also that two policemen had set up yellow police tape and established a make-shift perimeter. He hit the siren for a microsecond, giving a shrill burp which parted the spectators like crickets, and he pulled to the curb. Tall and reedy, Martik stretched his back as he emerged from the sedan. He removed his jacket, set it neatly on the passenger seat, grabbed his phone and scene kit, and looked over the spectators – some jockeyed for a better look and some reflexively stepped back.

One of the policemen held up the yellow tape, and Martik ducked under. He pulled an ID wallet from his pocket and flipped it open as he walked to the other patrolman on the scene. "Detective Martik," he announced, looking at the body lying on the sidewalk, still dripping and in a pool of water. He squinted in the dim light at the man's name on his uniform. "Officer Harrison, what can you tell me?" Without waiting for a reply, he pulled on his trouser legs and squatted over the body.

"Not too much, detective. The lady over there," he said, gesturing to a young woman seated on a metal chair against the wall of a small café, light scarf to her mouth and a dog's leash in her hand. The dog was curled up under the chair. "She called it in about 10 minutes ago. She yelled for help when she saw the body in the water and an older guy who was out crabbing ran over." Martik glanced up and noticed an older man wearing a faded Orioles cap and a gray well-worn sweatshirt hanging over khaki waders.

"Was the body on the sidewalk when you got here or in the water?"

"In the water. The dispatcher told the woman not to touch anything, and neither of them did. We got here and fished the guy out."

"Gloved?"

"Yes sir."

Martik reached for a pair of gloves from his scene kit as he leaned over the body. "Well, I doubt he came from the Cat's Tail Pub," he said, nodding to one of the bars across the street. "Not dressed like this." He pulled his phone from his pocket, clicked on the camera app, and tapped video. "Male, slender, six feet, maybe six two. Seems dressed well – gray slacks with matching jacket, dress shirt – pretty ragged." He paused, clicked off the video, and stood to face the patrolman. "Harrison, tell me about the face."

The patrolman glanced down at the body, grimaced and just as quickly looked back at Martik. "That's how

4

we found him, detective. Crabs, maybe – or gulls. Gulls can do that."

Martik exhaled and squatted once again, his phone recording. "Body generally intact, face and upper torso, where exposed from the ripped shirt, are decayed – or burned, or--" he glanced up at the patrolman, "perhaps predation." He pulled at the jacket and ran his hand over the man's pants. He poked gloved fingers into each pocket. "No wallet, no money, no ID," he glanced at the wrists, "no rings or watch." He squinted and looked more closely at what remained of the man's face. Slowly blowing out air, he looked off to the left – then shook his head and returned his attention to the body. "Bullet entry in rear of the head, puffing of bone and tissue – probable contact shot. No exit wound. Likely small-caliber weapon. Only one shoe, black dress shoe. Gray socks and--" Martik quickly clicked off the video and reached for his scene kit, removing a small plastic bag and a pair of long tweezers. He again tapped the video record button. "Appears to be a paper tucked in the sock." He carefully unfolded the paper, and took a picture of what was printed there. "Bagging paper, bag coded EB1."

Martik stood and signaled the second patrolman to join them. "Okay, let's start the canvas. Somebody heard something or saw something."

The patrolman who had just joined them said, "I'll start with the spectators – names and contact info. The Java Grill across the street is open – I'll go there next."

Martik nodded. "After that, go to the hotel on the other side of the dock. But before that, a coffee would be good."

A black, windowless van pulled up and two men exited, pushing a stretcher with a large sack folded on top. One had a camera over his shoulder. Martik nodded to the men, who went to work, taking photographs and recording information with the efficiency and speed gained from frequent practice. Within a few minutes, they had pulled the body onto the stretcher, zipped the bag from feet to head, and rolled it back to the van. Without a sound, the van moved from the curb onto the paving stones of Thames Street.

Martik pocketed his phone and pulled a small notebook from his back pocket, a small pencil tucked into the metal rings. He walked to the two silently waiting at the wall of the café. "Detective Martik. Ma'am. Sir. I need to speak with you both."

The older man in the baseball cap stood away from the wall. The woman with the scarf looked up from her chair, clutching her dog's leash.

From one of the rooms on the second floor of the luxury hotel across the water, the drapes were pulled back. The room was in darkness so no one could see the man watching the unfolding scene through binoculars. "Yes," he whispered. "Perfect." Closing the drapes, he turned to take a shower. He had an early plane to catch.

The red glow of the Dominos Sugar factory sign from across the harbor reflected off the still water.

Chapter 2:
Three days earlier

"Non, rien de rien. Non, je ne regrette rien. Ni le bien, qu'on m'a fait, ni le mal, tout ce m'est bien egale." The plaintive sound of Edith Piaf's voice from the boat ahead of him resonating in his native language, reminded Luc Benoit of the irony of the lyrics. Luc leaned against the "Private residence" sign at the end of the gravel road, taking one long look back to see if there was any sign of another vehicle on the cross street above. and relieved to note that, even on a Friday afternoon, there appeared to be no traffic on the narrow road. His crisp and creased silhouette was nearly obscured by the trunks of Cyprus trees and thick bushes. As he listened. Piaf was singing, *"No, absolutely nothing, I regret nothing. Not the good that has been given, Not the bad. It's all the same to me."*

"Irony," Luc said to himself, "I regret everything."

He pushed aside the brush where he had parked, looking over at the dark blue pickup pulled under a Cyprus on the side and noting that there were spots of rust over the wheels. This had to be Jake's second vehicle. Work truck, he thought, knowing that Jake would never tolerate rust on any car he drove to the art museum or university. Two steps through a patch of mud and he was on the wooden dock. When the second plank groaned and leaned, he grasped at the gray, hardboard rectangle that had been gripped tightly under his arm and held it high over his head, skip-stepping to the next plank – which seemed to hold.

Checking the black nylon straps on the thin crate, he tucked it securely under his arm and walked gingerly down the dock onto the gangway, pulling a scrap of paper from the pocket of his navy-blue blazer and pushing curly, dark blonde hair from his forehead with his sleeve - wishing he had worn something more disposable. Staring at the address written there and at the damaged and aging houseboat ahead of him he shook his head. The lines of the boat were elegant and much of the fine old trim was still visible. But he could more readily see the past in this structure than he could the future. The low, flat deck was strong, but covered with equipment and the filth of reconstruction. The cabin curved at the bow, with a handsome filigree that was visible on one side even though it was missing from the other. Crusted metal was cleaned and polished in test patches, revealing a richly ornamented brass history that perhaps could impress again one day, especially if the dark woodwork could also be redeemed. Intriguing, he thought. To find this address, he had passed the most recognized (and most traveled) marinas along the Chesapeake Bay, and then to the lesser-known and seedier locations, and then finally to this. The cabin sported a large rectangular window in the front and three circular windows along the side. Two of these were missing glass and were covered with heavy plastic.

Unbuttoning his jacket for better maneuverability, Luc walked carefully toward the boat, carrying the crate by its nylon handle and hoping the old boards would hold. Several of the wooden boards looked tenuous, and his long legs allowed him to easily step over them. He arrived to where a metal plank, at one time painted red but now mostly scuffed base metal, connected the dock to the boat deck. Black gripping strips had been recently glued to the metal.

"Jake?" he shouted. Hearing nothing, he stepped onto the deck, impressed that the boat didn't shift on his arrival. He half expected his presence would tilt the thing, inviting the thick gray water of the bay onto the deck. "Jake!" he repeated. There was still no answer, but the music continued from somewhere inside and he stepped into the large cabin interior. The inside of the cabin, like the exterior, was a battle of old elegance and recent disrepair – excavated walls around brass fittings and oiled teakwood trim. The smell of solvent and wood oil rasped at his nostrils as he stepped forward. One wall had been refinished, varnished and polished, and on that wall hung a painting - small amber brush strokes catching the breeze of a mustard-yellow meadow wrapped in a square of blue and green poplars. He smiled, knowing that, despite all he was seeing, at least he was in the right place. "Lily," he whispered. "Here you are." The immediate effect was of warmth and the rich smell of light rain on an early-summer afternoon. It was also a bittersweet fragrance of another time – a better time.

"Jake, where the hell are you?"

There was a creaking below his feet, the music stopped, and a hatch cover rose -- visible around a partial wall in the far corner of the cabin. An imposing figure, solidly-framed, emerged and unbent himself to stand erect, nearly disguised in oil and rusty grime. Once again, Luc wasn't sure he had the right place, although he did recognize the reddish-brown hair, curling with dirt and matted like some rainforest undergrowth. The man stopped and glared, hefting a large pipe wrench menacingly in his hand, biceps clearly flexed and pushing against the confines of a blackened tee-shirt. Rattling noises emerged from the open hatch, and without turning his stare, the man reached back with his foot and kicked the hatch cover closed with a metallic crash. Both men stood silently.

Luc waved at the expanse of the houseboat. "Nice place." He attempted a grin.

"How the hell did you find me?" Jake asked in a low growl nearly indistinguishable from the sound below of an engine clinging to life.

"Come on, yours was not a difficult trail." Luc waited for a response, but getting none, he raised one palm in surrender. "I knew you were back in Baltimore. Your father is still at the Walters gallery, and your mother is still teaching at MICA. He was out of the country, but your mother gave me your location and sent me here. You aren't really that hard to find." He took a tentative step forward. "At least your mother was happy to see me."

Jake stood silently, still unblinking through the filth. "There's a lot she doesn't know."

Luc paused, hearing the line as both a statement and a warning. "It's been a long time. Much to think about." He nodded in the direction of the painting. "I recognize the meadow at the canal in Troyes."

"Why are you here?" Jake said. "What do you want? You look like a fucking businessman."

"I want a few minutes of your time. To catch up, and to ask for one favor – perhaps for old times' sake, and perhaps because I'm very close to being a dead businessman."

Jake shook his head and exhaled, looking at the deck. "Of course you are," he said. He set the wrench on the deck, pulled a plastic deck chair over and motioned Luc to sit. "I'm getting some coffee." As he walked to the cabin door, a large dog emerged from the brush behind them as if had been part of the shadows. Its face signaled husky – or perhaps part akita. Its coat, a brindled brown with a white frame around fiercely attentive eyes, caught a flash of sun as it trotted along the dock and onto the boat, stopping suddenly to glare at the stranger – slight curl to the white fur over his mouth. Luc felt his pulse quicken. "Bromo, lie down," Jake called from the cabin. "You are one hell of a watchdog. Anyway, don't get Mr. future-dead-businessman's suit dirty."

"I appreciate the gesture," Luc said as the dog flopped on the deck, licking some of the mud from its paws.

"Don't get your hopes up," Jake replied, dipping a clean cloth into a basin and wiping away much of the filth from his hands and face. "I may still throw you into the bay myself." Stepping into a half-renovated galley area, he noticed a drawer half open, revealing an orange bottle of pills and quietly pushed the drawer closed.

As he waited, Luc looked again to the painting on the wall. He noticed it was carefully covered in glass, and sealed at the edges of the frame to protect it from weather. A few minutes later Jake emerged, two tall French press cylinders and two empty mugs in his hands. The smell of a strong French roast was suddenly everywhere. "Ahh," Luc murmured. "Still have a taste for the finer things, I see."

Jake slid into a second deck chair and slowly plunged the press, pouring himself a cup of the aromatic brew. Without looking up, he reprised his question. "So why are you here? What's going on?"

"Five years, Jake. Five years can be a long time." He sipped his coffee and spoke quietly, looking into the mug. "Things have changed. Things have happened." Then he looked up and his face brightened for a moment. "And look at you," he said, gesturing with an open palm. "Talk about change! You have turned things around. You have quite a reputation in--"

"What do you know about my reputation?" An accusation rather than a question. "I left Paris in a very bad place. I've worked hard to put a new life together. Is that about to be pulled apart? Again?"

"No, of course not. But I need to know if I can still trust you. I can't apologize any more for your hand. I wish I could, but--"

Jake set his coffee mug on the deck. "It's not about my hand – it never was. That's history – and what I did in Paris I did of my own free will. It was my decision.

Every part of it." He shifted in the chair, trying to quiet his rising anger.

"No, no, that isn't what I meant. I mean that you've had to re-build your life. It's a good thing – a great thing, really. I searched for you online and you do have a highly-regarded reputation you know. I learned that you were able to paint again. In fact, you have become very good again – perhaps better than ever. I am sorry that you can't show or sell your work. Truly sorry." Luc paused deliberately and sipped. "The coffee – thank you for this." He shifted in the chair, making sure the crate was resting securely by his leg. "I stayed in one place, it seems. I still work in galleries - although I've moved around a bit and up that ladder. But you! You were able to begin again - to reinvent yourself! Lecturing around the world and organizing art conservation labs. Google knows you quite well! I saw you listed in Berlin, Moscow, Budapest. So many cities and so many museums. But never the Louvre, never the d'Orsay, never the Centre Pompidou. Never Paris." He let the statement hang with the unspoken question.

Jake stared into a space beyond his old friend.

Luc looked again at the painting. "She would have taken you back, you know. In a heartbeat."

Jake's eyes suddenly snapped forward. "Enough. What's this all about? Start talking."

"I need you to hold something for me for just a few days. I have to speak with someone and then I'll come back and tell you everything. It will all be over then. So will you do this for me?"

Jake looked at the boarded crate leaning against Luc's leg, recognizing it as transport for a canvas. "Why not just rent a storage locker someplace?"

"Because I'm being pretty closely watched." The statement hung in silence. "Will you do this for me?"

"No, I won't."

"Look Jake, as a friend," the word was a question. "I'm asking you because I need someone I can really trust – or at least used to trust. Only for a few days and then I can tell you everything. But I can't right now."

"Are you in trouble?"

"Yes, but I won't be when I see you again."

"Is this illegal?"

"Yes, but not for very long."

Jake looked at Luc and at the crate. He looked away and then back again. "Can I look inside?"

"I would really rather you didn't. I need you to keep this in hiding." Luc waited a beat and added, "Only for a few days. Then it will all be clear. I promise you."

Jake stood and reached out his hand. Luc handed him the nylon handle of the crate.

"Thank you. You won't regret it." Luc reached to shake Jake's hand, but when it wasn't offered, he turned to leave.

Jake turned to the cabin and held up the small crate. "I already regret it," he said.

Chapter 3:
Douai France, October 16, 1918

Private Otis Wilson raised his head, spitting and coughing the mud that had pushed into his mouth, eyes, and ears when he fell. His ears were ringing from the explosion, and he barely heard the other shells falling. He couldn't clear one eye, but was able to see from the other and strained to look around. Holding a finger to each nostril, he blew the mud from his nose and immediately twisted his face at the onrush of acrid smoke and the thick sweetness of burnt blood. The church which had seemed to offer cover and safety had provided neither, and in fact resembled more a quarry pile of stone than a structure. Large sections of timber from the roof were scattered, one falling horrifyingly close by and crushing the skull of another man in uniform. In the mud and destruction, Wilson couldn't make out who the unfortunate soldier had been, although it perhaps was Harrison – the young teacher from Cornwall with all the great history stories. He thought to remove the identification tag which had been issued to all soldiers only a few months earlier, following the instructions from his company commander, and then noticed that the scene before him was littered with the rest of his company. He struggled to recognize faces of his comrades, but couldn't seem to tell one mud-covered body from the next. The British had apparently taken a heavy blow on this one. He walked to two other bodies to check for life, but found none. Trying to think of their names, he found he could only recall a very few. Harrison, of course, and another – he thought might be Blake, or maybe it was Blackstone – something like that. His thinking seemed as muddied as his surroundings. He had never been good with faces.

Or with other people, for that matter.

The town of Douai had fallen to the Bosch easily in the early days of the war. Just 13 miles separated this small coal-mining center in northern France from the Belgian border and its factories were a coveted target of the advancing Germans. Moving into France had seemed relatively simple after their grueling march through Belgium, facing a heroic, yet overmatched collection of Belgian troops and local police forces. Now, four years later, the advancing British and French troops were re-claiming some of these early casualty towns. Wilson, unable to always "keep his head down," had seen the general outline of the town from the hill to the south. It seemed ghost-like, some buildings still standing, some with walls, roofs, or corners in ruin, and some completely obliterated by bombardments and counter-bombardments that had lasted for more than a week. The town center now resembled a cratered rugby field – nothing taller than a few feet left standing. And yet, just to the left of the former town center stood a church - seemingly intact. A single stone tower, rising perhaps two stories above other standing buildings, indicated a structure likely more than two centuries old. A few windows had been blown out, but from the hill it was clear that the structure was sound. A large arched entrance was open and unblocked by rubble, providing easy access as the company ran to escape ground fire. As Wilson and the others entered the church, the hammering sounds of battle muffled and seemed distant. The men looked around at their new shelter, noting the open simplicity of the nave and strength of its massive vertical columns - three on each side. A small wooden rood screen separated the nave from the chancel. The company, seemingly in unison and without orders, lifted off their packs and headed to the several open window areas, hoisting rifles to scan for the enemy. Breathing was heavy and talking seemed to cease. After a moment, Wilson, positioned at a rear corner of the nave, could hear some orders, but these too were muffled. He turned to Harrison on his left and grinned at their good fortune. Harrison smiled back. A sudden crash was accompanied by a lifting of the ground beneath them, and followed by several more explosions. A flash temporarily blinded him, and the muffled orders became shouts. Wilson saw some troops scrambling for new positions, and then heard a groaning and cracking from overhead. He neither saw nor heard anything else.

Now, listening for anyone to call out or cry for help as the ringing in his ears lessened, Wilson noticed that the battle seemed to have moved significantly to his left somewhere. Without any context for location, he had no idea whether that indicated advance or retreat, nor could he understand how much time had passed since his unit had rushed the edge of the village and sought cover in the church, only to have everything go black in the wrenching concussions and collapse of the roof.

Struggling to move without support and turning to survey his situation, Wilson noted that the remaining structures of the church, like the rest of the town and, in fact, his immediate world, was painted over in the same muddy brown – looking much like the sepia-toned photographs he had seen of so many French villages and rural scenes. He noticed a crater next to a corner of the church that still seemed to be intact. "Any crump-hole in a storm," he mumbled and staggered over to flop in the hole. He picked up a rifle from the mud, and examined the damaged barrel jammed with debris. "Spiked," he grunted, tossing it aside. He checked the service revolver at his belt, and brushed the mud from its grip.

"Hey, there!" he yelled, not recognizing the harsh crack of his own voice. "Hey there!"

Rapid gunfire answered from far off to the left.

Looking around at the intact corner of the church, Wilson caught the glimmer of something inside a glass case – the glass cracked but unbroken and lying half buried in dirt and debris. He reached over and brushed off the case, seeing gold artifacts inside. Not a religious man, Wilson had no idea what the objects might be, but they were clearly of some value. Looking around once more, he smashed the glass and wrapped the gold items in a cloth from his kit pouch, snapping them into the pouch attached to his belt. Then he saw the painting.

"Anybody alive here?" he yelled once more into the smoke. Hearing no reply, he walked over to the wall from where the painting had fallen. Its glass front was smashed, but the frame and canvas seemed intact. Wilson's short stint in university at Staffordshire just before the war seemed from another lifetime, but he had always enjoyed his art history lectures, and recognized that this was not merely an amateurish sketch from some favorite parishioner. He lifted the painting and looked it over closely, brushing off the lower corners to see if he could spot a name. In the darkness of the right corner, he could make out "COROT" in capital letters. "Corot," Wilson said in a whisper. "Really?" He knew of Corot's work.

And of its worth.

"Allo!" Wilson heard from his left, following by a fit of coughing. "Bloody Hell, Allo!"

Wilson went instinctively to the revolver at his side and turned. Squinting, he could make out a form struggling to get to its knees. "Who is it?" he called into the smoke.

"Sergeant Cavanaugh," the voice replied, sounding more annoyed than hurt. "And you?"

"Private Wilson," he said as he stepped to the squatting man, recognizing his bushy mustache and round face – usually reddish but now, like everything else, browned over with mud. He offered a hand to lift him to his feet, but the sergeant's knees buckled and he fell again.

"Ankle's off," the sergeant muttered angrily.

Wilson looked and noticed that, in fact, the sergeant's ankle had been blown off completely. He was surprised to notice that the sergeant had already tied off the stump with a piece of rope. "Just sit there, sir," he said. "I'll find a medic."

"Hold up, Wilson," Cavanaugh said. "What's our situation?"

Wilson looked around once more, still squinting with his one good eye. "Pretty badly done, sir," he offered. "We may be the only two alive here."

"Any reconnaissance?" The sergeant twisted and grunted, "Bloody Hell."

Wilson looked around. "No chance, sir." He paused and added, "Nothing much left. There are some relics and a painting here, though." He immediately regretted his words.

"Valuables?" the sergeant asked. "Have to secure those. Prevent looting." The sergeant arched his back as if stretching from a night's sleep. "Go find a medic, and get someone here to list and secure the valuables." After a moment of silence, he added, "Best get moving, private."

"Yes sir," Private Otis Wilson said, turning to walk away. He walked three steps, paused, turned, removed his handgun from his belt, and fired three times into the chest of the sergeant.

Chapter 4

Jake was sitting on the deck of his houseboat, reading the Sunday Sun with a cup of coffee and the company of Bromo, and deciding which of the many projects he would begin in his never-ending restoration. It had been almost two years since he had seen the derelict boat advertised and realized immediately how grand it had once been. Although the restoration only marginally involved skills he had learned as an art conservationist, he was drawn to the idea of seeing again what this craft had once been. The work continued to be difficult, and stretched his understanding of everything from woodworking to engine repair, but he found a kind of quiet in it. There was a sort of Zen moment – like a runner's high – from the physical routine and slow progress. The vessel had been broken in so many ways, it would have been easy just to pass by and give it up as lost. He remembered, however, how broken he had once been, and his own slow journey from scrap. "I'll bring you back," he once said to the boat – and it seemed the filthier and more calloused his hands became, the more he meant it. The solitude of Sunday mornings was especially treasured, and he occasionally even spent Saturday night on the boat, rather than returning to his condo in Fell's Point.

He had even pushed aside the turmoil of his encounter with Luc, until he saw the black sedan pull up to the dock. It was unmarked, but he could make out the municipal license plate from his deck chair. He folded the paper and set it aside, taking one final sip of his coffee. "Shit," he mumbled to Bromo, "I knew it was going to be something." He stood to wipe his jeans, and realizing they were already stained, painted, and greased beyond any attempt at cleanliness, he set his coffee mug on a nearby packing crate and grabbed a rag from the deck.

After a long minute, a man opened the door and unfolded himself from the driver's seat. Stretching to his full height after some time confined in the car, he receded to a slight stoop - more from weariness than poor posture. From the deck, Jake noted that the man looked somehow used up, moving as if at the end of a long and exhausting shift. He pulled a gray nylon jacket from the car, and after removing a black breast wallet from the pocket, placed it carefully back in the car. He walked down the dock to the gangplank, ignoring the aging wood planks, and held up the wallet, displaying a shield and photo ID. "Detective Martik. Can I come aboard?"

"Sure." Jake said. He motioned Bromo into the boat's cabin. "What can I do for you?"

"Can I get your name?"

Jake tilted his head, pausing as he looked at the detective and pushing the thick reddish-brown curly hair to the side of his forehead. "Jake Daniels. My turn now - what's going on?"

Martik paused and apparently made a decision. "Mr. Daniels. I need you to come to Central Station. Voluntarily, of course."

Jake paused. "Uh-huh, but that doesn't really answer my question." He waved a hand to his surroundings. "We're a long way from The Block here. Why Central Station?"

Martik looked down to the deck and nodded slightly. "Because Central is the location of my office, Mr. Daniels." He paused and added, "I'm hoping you can help identify a body."

Jake felt his pulse quicken, but fought down any visible reaction. "Detective, when you arrived, you didn't even know my name. You had to ask. So what makes you think I can be of any help?"

"We found a piece of paper on the person of a young man pulled from the harbor this morning. This address was on the paper. There were no other personal items, and we were hoping you could be of some help."

Jake looked to the overgrown brush that shielded his houseboat from all but the most determined passersby. He listened, but there were no sounds except the lapping of the water and a few morning insects. He heard a low magnolia branch scrape against the cabin behind him and remembered that he was going to trim that back today. After that, he was going to take a look at the bilge pump. It had every appearance of a terrific Sunday. "I'll meet you there as soon as I can. I would like to clean up and secure the dock. Then I'll get to the station. I'll be there in about an hour. Since this is voluntary, I assume that's okay?"

Martik pushed the wallet and shield he had been holding into his pants pocket and turned. "That would be fine, Mr. Daniels. Thanks for your cooperation. The Central Station is on—"

"I know where it is. Let me get cleaned up and I'll get there as soon as I can. Probably an hour."

Martik turned to leave, speaking over his shoulder. "I'll alert the front desk, and have someone direct you to my office. An hour would be fine." With that, he walked to the dock, off to the gravel parking area and into his car.

Watching him pull away, Jake looked down at the deck and exhaled, as if he had just stopped holding his breath. He entered the cabin to see Bromo sprawled on the bed that they sometimes shared, his large gray head turned to the side and his four paws in the air. Bromo rolled, sat up and watched as Jake walked to the bed and, reaching behind the mattress, slipped a small section of paneling aside. The hardboard rectangle was still there behind the panel. He stared at it for a moment, then pushed the panel back into place. Shit," he said, and then louder, "SHIT!" His right hand began to ache and he shook it to quiet the sensation. Grabbing a wallet, and a set of keys, he held the cabin door open. "Come on, Bromo. Time to do your business."

Chapter 5

Pulling his pickup into a spot along Calvert Street next to a newly-created green space, Jake walked back one block to Central Police Station on East Baltimore Street – more commonly known as "the Block." Parking on Calvert was marginally safer from vandalism than at any of the available spots on the Block itself, named as Baltimore's most infamous "adult strip" of clubs and bars – ironically located across the street and one block down from the central police headquarters. Of course, the real irony, Jake thought, was the idea that anyone would vandalize his "workhorse" pickup. As he crossed onto East Baltimore Street, he heard shouting from a bar called Cranston's, diagonally across from the station entrance. A heavy-set man, Ravens cap askew on his balding head, staggered out, yelling at another who followed him onto the sidewalk. As the shouting escalated, two patrol officers who had been leaning against their car talking stopped to look - readying for trouble. However, after a few more outbursts of expletives too incoherent to make out, the heavy man adjusted his cap, turned and staggered slowly away, still gesturing and weaving. The officers relaxed and continued their conversation.

Walking to the three tall glass doors that marked the entrance of headquarters, Jake looked up to see the four-story square block of a building, unadorned on this front side by any windows or decorative markings.

Central Station from the front was simply a wall of concrete – solid, tough, and unwelcoming. The US flag hung from one side of the entrance, and the checkered Maryland flag from the other - red, white, and blue flanked by yellow and black. Stars and Stripes next to the heraldic banner of Sir George Calvert, First Lord Baltimore. The Maryland flag was at half-mast, and Jake recalled a recent story of a police officer shot on duty. Going through the center door, he paused in front of the metal detector at the front desk. A middle-aged woman in uniform, stocky but intimidatingly firm, looked up from the Sunday paper. "Help you?"

"Detective Martik's office?"

The woman tilted her head and looked at him. "Name?"

"Jake Daniels."

She pulled a clipboard over and flipped a few pages. "Right. Okay. Go through the detector and to the end of the hall. You'll see the sign." She reached behind her and handed Jake a plastic bin. "Everything from your pockets in here. Belt too." With that, she nodded to her right to a man standing next to the metal detector, picked up a desk phone, and punched a few numbers. "Daniels," was all she said, although Jake noticed her waiting as something was said in reply.

"Loud outside," Jake said to the man as he re-buckled his belt.

The man sniffed dismissively. "Cranston's," he said, shaking his head. And that was apparently all that needed to be said. "End of the hall. Down one flight to the temporary morgue."

"Temporary?" Jake said, trying to dampen his breathing with the question.

"Yea. While they do renovations at East Quarters."

At the end of the hall, Jake noticed the sign at the stairway, directing him to the morgue one flight down. The stairway was walled in cinderblock and painted in an off-white gloss. Black metal steps led down, and Jake paused at the bottom in front of a windowless swinging door. Jake could feel the muscles tighten at the back of his jaw as he clenched his teeth, pushed and walked through.

Two steps into an austere concrete-walled room, painted in the same off-white gloss, he froze. He wanted to say, "Son-Of-A-Bitch!" He wanted to say, "What-The-Fuck!"

What he said was, "Lily." More resignation than a question or comment.

Her small frame was half turned to him as he entered the morgue, but her wild auburn curly hair was unmistakable, despite her attempt to capture and tie it into submission. She was impeccably dressed in gray jacket and slacks - as if for a corporate meeting. Upon hearing him call her name she turned completely. "Jake," she said softly.

Jake looked ahead to see the far wall, solid except for a large glass next to an open door. Detective Martik was visible through the glass, standing next to a metal table draped with a dark cloth and speaking to a young man in green scrubs. He suddenly felt unable to move, and spoke to Lily's back. "What are you doing here? I thought you were in Paris."

"I just got here. We can talk more later."

"Not sure I want to do that."

Lily turned quickly back to face him. "No. We will talk."

"Mr. Daniels. Ms. O'Connell," Martik leaned back to the open door and spoke to get their attention. "Could you come over here to the window?" Not looking at each other, but rather to the shape on the table, both Jake and Lily moved forward. "I'm going to remove the cloth and ask if either of you know this man," Martik said from the other side of the glass. "Before I do, however, I want you to understand that he was found in the harbor, and has not been cosmetically altered in any way. There is some facial damage. Do you both understand?"

Jake nodded. "Yes, detective," Lily said.

Slowly, Martik pulled the cloth from the man's face. Lily lifted her head and said something Jake could not hear, while Jake looked at the floor, shaking his head. Martik replaced the cloth.

"The face isn't quite clear through the glass," Jake said. "Can you pull the sheet down a bit?" Lily looked over at him, eyebrows raised slightly as Martik pulled she sheet back from the torso. "His name is Lucas Benoit," he added, after a pause.

"Yes," Lily said. "It is."

Martik stepped out of the room and closed the door behind him. He paused and looked at them both. "Ms. O'Connell, we have already spoken briefly, but I'll need to continue our conversation."

Lily nodded. "Certainly, detective. You have my complete cooperation."

Jake turned to look quizzically at Lily, when Martik spoke to him. "Mr. Daniels, I will also have questions for you. But I'm starting with this one."

Jake looked back to the detective. "What?"

"Both just now and when I first spoke to you at your houseboat, you didn't show any shock or even surprise. I think you knew what you would find here today. Am I wrong?"

Jake looked at the cloth covering Luc's body, noticing a small brown stain near the feet - an old stain that had not washed white, left from another day, another tragedy. He also registered the odor of the entire basement area - not of antiseptic or some chemical smell, as he had anticipated, but more a smell of oily age, of mold and damp and heavy acceptance of sorrow.

"Am I wrong?

Jake looked up at Martik, thinking to tell him that he, in fact, couldn't have been more wrong. "No, you aren't wrong. Luc came to see me Friday morning. I hadn't seen him in five years, which is why he had my address on the paper. We didn't really talk, and he said he would be back in a few days to catch up, but he seemed on edge. There isn't really any more to it than that."

"Were you and Mr. Benoit friends?"

With this, Lily looked over and up at Jake's face, which continued to be expressionless.

"No," Jake said after a brief pause. "Colleagues at one time. Shared an apartment in Paris, but not friends."

Lily's head drooped slightly and she looked away.

"I'll need you both to stick around for a while. I do have questions for both of you, and I'm assuming that presents no problems?" The question was clearly not a question, and the request was clearly not a request. Jake and Lily both nodded.

Martik's small office was on the 2nd floor, and they took the stairs. Jake noticed that the elevator was temporarily undergoing some sort of maintenance, although no one seemed to be currently working. Martik picked up on Jake's glance. "Work continues on Monday. No real need for time-and-a-half for Sundays. Ms. O'Connell, if you could have a seat here," he motioned to a bench in the hallway, "I want to start with Mr. Daniels."

Twenty minutes later Jake emerged and Martik motioned for Lily to enter. Jake and Lily exchanged a wordless glance and she turned, Martik closing his door behind her. Jake was about to leave when he saw a paper left of the bench, blank except for a phone number. He paused, sighed, leaned over, and took the paper with one swiping motion - somewhat hostile, somewhat resigned.

Chapter 6

Leadbetter's Tavern was the last of the famous dive bars in the seedy-turned-chic Fell's Point neighborhood, and it certainly looked the part. Always known for its live music, the cloudy glass front was covered with taped up fliers of musical acts for this night, the week ahead, and the two or three months already past. There had been a time when Sunday evenings would have been packed, but no more. The room was half filled, mostly with familiar faces. Through the maze of fliers on the window, Jake could see Lily outside, with black jeans and a white tailored blouse, her dark red hair brushed into soft waves that broke over her shoulders. "Damn," he said, remembering all he had worked so long to forget. He saw her hesitate and double-check the name over the door; then she pushed the door inward, looked to see Jake, and walked in, gliding with a confidence he had always admired. She motioned to the bartender as she walked by, pointing to one of the tap levers, and walked over to the table where Jake was seated.

"What?" she asked, seeing a smile as she pulled out the chair across from him at the small round table.

He looked down at his drink, shaking his head slowly. "Have you been here before?"

Lily looked around. The pictures on the wall were faded, photographs shifting colors as they aged, some behind glass so smoky the picture was clouded into obscurity – or perhaps just into history. Smoking hadn't been allowed for a decade, but the smell of cigarettes was woven into the patchwork fabric of beer and scotch. Nevertheless, the bar itself, Lily noted, was immaculate dark mahogany and polished brass. Over in the corner, an older man, balding despite his attempt to tie his long fringe hair into a tail, picked up a well-used Martin guitar, its face nearly worn through, and began to tune - smiling and chatting with those sitting nearby. He could have been the ghost of Leadbetter himself, or John Lee Hooker, or Mississippi John Hurt, or any of the hundreds of blues acts from the tavern's past. There was a background buzz of quiet conversations - of people in small groups who liked to drink quietly, talk quietly, and enjoy the company of this extended family. Everyone seemed to know everyone. A few looked at Lily, but none for more than a moment. "No. But I had a colleague in DC who used to swear by this place."

"Swear by it or swear in it?" Jake asked, still smiling.

"Both, I'm sure." A middle-aged woman set a pilsner glass of beer in front of Lily, in exchange for the few bills she had just set on the table. She took a sip, looking over the glass at Jake. "So why didn't they name this Leadbelly's?"

Jake nodded. "Impressive, and you got the history right. This was named after Leadbelly. However, his real name was Huddie Leadbetter. And this has always been a place where older performers can remind us of what good music really is, and where younger players can perform in front of an appreciative audience.

Seems to be on its last legs, however," he added, looking around. "Word is somebody just bought it to turn it into another Fell's Point cocktail bar or gift shop or something. Too bad."

Lily took another sip and pushed her glass to the side. "So how do we begin this?"

Jake shifted back slightly, leaning away. "Okay. Let's start with the most obvious -- what are you doing here?"

Lily looked so intently into Jake's eyes that he had to force himself not to look away. "I was following Luc."

Jake sipped at his stout, considering her response. "But that doesn't really answer, does it?" Jake looked at her. "Why. Why were you following him and what kind of trouble is he in?"

Lily's full and perfectly-shaped auburn eyebrows raised and her gaze became as hot as it was cold. "Was." A pause. "You mean 'was' he in. And it's complicated."

Jake let it pass. "So what's going on here?"

Lily looked away, and he wondered whether she would say more. "A lot has changed in five years," she began.

No shit, Jake thought, shifting uncomfortably. "I'm guessing you aren't a student at the Sorbonne anymore. So exactly what are you?"

Lily looked at Jake, seeking someone who didn't seem to be there anymore. "A dual major in art history and criminal justice, even from someplace as well-regarded as the Sorbonne, doesn't open many doors.

However, the doors it does open, it opens pretty wide. I interned at the FBI during an art fraud investigation and apparently impressed the Bureau. They hired me a few months later."

"So you're FBI?"

"Specialist. Art Crimes unit. Money laundering. Art theft."

Jake nodded, fighting back an anger that peered at him through an unopened door to an unexplored room in his head. "So are you stationed in the states now?"

"European division; I'm still in Paris," Lily said. "Most of our cases are international."

"Your languages come in handy, then. How many now?"

"Still five."

The anger rose again, and he fought it back. "And Luc?"

"Something wasn't right about the auction house where he was working. Actually, managing for the last two years. He moved up that ladder. He knew something was wrong. Then... well things got worse." She took a sip, put down her glass and shook her head slowly. "Dammit, Jake, what did you mean you 'weren't friends'? That's bullshit and you know it! You were like brothers!"

"What kind of trouble is, or was he in?" he repeated.

"No!" Lily said, voice rising slightly, "My turn. What happened to you? Did you think nothing would change in five years? We should be crying together right now! And you--" she held her hands open to him as if offering communion, "What is wrong with you? Aren't you feeling anything?"

Jake considered the question. He should have been in touch with Lily over those years. None of this was her fault, he knew. Of course, she could have tried to contact him, as well. "It's complicated at this end too, Lily," he replied. "But let's be honest – you're carrying a pretty large chip on those shoulders. And you still aren't telling me everything."

"No, I'm not. But since we're being so honest, neither are you. And about that chip? You have no idea."

Jake nodded, considered the knot in his gut, took a long last swallow of his stout, and put the glass down. "Did you drive?"

Lily paused and her breathing slowed. "No. I'm at a hotel over in East Harbor. I walked."

"I want to take you someplace. We can talk there."

As the performer leaned toward his microphone and opened a soft blues riff, Lily took one last sip of beer and pushed the half-finished glass forward. "Let's go then."

On Sunday evening, the drive over to Point Breeze and Colgate Creek went smoothly, and was generally silent, each realizing that their conversation with all of its heat had to resume at some point. Jake made a few comments on old architecture as they passed by and Lily pretended to notice, asking about the scenery when his commentary slowed. In about 20 minutes, they turned onto a gravel roadway which meandered down to the bayside dock. Jake stopped in front of his houseboat and nodded for Lily to get out and follow him to the dock.

"Careful on the dock," he said. "Needs some work."

They were silent as they stepped onto the boat deck. Immediately, they could hear a plaintive whine from behind the cabin door. "Watch yourself," Jake added, opening the cabin door. The dog came bounding out in giant leaps. "Slow, Bromo!" Jake said in a staccato tone that the dog immediately obeyed - walking carefully to Lily, tail wagging and the black tip of his nose pointing in hope of a new friend and perhaps a face-rub. She immediately crouched, petting and cooing with a voice that Jake suddenly longed to hear again. Bromo's large ears, white with brown trim, flattened on his head and his gray eyes closed.

"He's a charmer!" she said, scratching Bromo's head.

"No argument there," Jake said. "Okay, Bromo, go do it."

The dog pranced off the dock and into the bushes, emerging moments later relieved and ready for more attention. Lily, who had been scanning the deck, turned again to pet the dog. "What a gorgeous coat! Is he part Husky by any chance?" She pushed her hand down the thick brown and white fur of his back while the dog gave her arm a tentative lick. "How long have you had him?"

"Yes, he is part Husky, I'm pretty sure. The rest is, well, the rest. We found each other when I bought this boat, and I think he's lived here longer than I have. I had the title papers in my hand and was walking around assessing where to begin re-habbing when this mutt bounded from the bushes into the water and up on the dock. He came at me looking for trouble, and I was looking around for something to fend him off when he stopped dead and sat – just looking at me. We stared at each other for a minute and then he walked over for attention. I cleaned him up and we got in the truck to report him to animal services in town. They run a kill shelter and so I decided to keep him. The shelter is across the street from the Bromo Seltzer Tower so he got named." The dog walked over to a blanket on the deck and curled up, his tail flicking as he looked up at the new visitor. "He's pretty special."

Lily stepped around the deck, taking in the general disrepair, and noticing the elegant trim and possibilities. "This is wonderful! I mean, it could be. What a treasure. So you live here? I mean, actually live here?"

"It's a work in progress. I have a condo back at Fell's Point, but this is a hobby." Jake opened the cabin door and motioned Lily inside.

"This," Lily began with a wave of her arm, "reminds me of the houseboats on the Seine - especially that one just around the bend from Pont Alma - the 'fixer-upper' as you so diplomatically put it. Well anyway," she continued, "it fits you somehow, and it does have amazing poss—" As her eyes found the painting on the wall, she froze.

Jake pulled the plastic chair to the center of the room, followed her stare, and pretended not to notice it, and also not to notice the way her shoulders rose and fell as she breathed quickly. "Here. Sit for a minute. I have to show you something." Without speaking or taking her eyes off the painting, Lily sat. Jake moved through a doorway to the next room and reappeared carrying the crate. He sat on the other plastic chair.

"What's that?" Lily asked, refocusing her attention on the container.

"Luc left it here last Friday. He told me not to look, but I think we both know what's inside."

Lily stared first at the crate, then at Jake, and then to the crate again. "Have you opened it?"

Jake shook his head. "Nope. But whatever is in there is why you're here. Right?"

Lily paused, then nodded.

"So is it stolen?"

Lily shrugged. "I don't know."

Jake stood and pulled a folding table from the wall, extending its legs and setting it upright. "Let's find out." He cut some packing tape that had sealed the edges, loosened the nylon support straps, pried one side loose with a screwdriver, and pulled back on the top. "Oh for Christ sake!"

Lily gasped. "Oh, Luc," she whispered.

Jake leaned over and squinted. "Pissarro? Really?"

Lily stood and looked closely, examining carefully the signature in the lower right corner. "Could be - or a good imitation. Knowing Luc's talents and habits, I'm guessing it's a forgery."

"Then he's gotten much better. I don't like the thought of that." Jake looked over at Lily. "I know what you're going to say -- you're going to say, 'I need to take this with me,' and be off to Paris - or wherever. But that's not going to happen."

"Jake, you can't stop me."

"Actually, I can. Sorry, but he left that with me for safekeeping, and I'm not letting it go until I know what's going on, and you aren't helping with your shortened stories and half-truths." Lily looked up, anger firing her eyes. "I'm not saying you're lying – but I am saying that you aren't telling me everything. This is all too neat, and we both know that is never how it is. The last thing I wanted was to be involved in anything, but I am. He left that with me and now he's dead. It doesn't stop now – it can't. Besides, by the time you get some sort of warrant, I'll have hidden it away." Jake looked at Lily's frown, as she moved her gaze from the canvas to his eyes. "Look, somebody killed him, and like it or not, I'm part of this now." Jake replaced the cover on the crate and tapped it back into place. "If we can't figure out what to do, then OK, I'll let you take it with you."

"What do you mean 'we'? Look, Jake, there is no 'we' anymore."

"Let's get back in the car. I want to take this back to my condo and figure out what to do." He handed the crate to Lily. "On good faith, right? Bromo. Ride!" The dog perked up and pranced to the end of the dock and waited. Visibly disappointed when Jake opened the rear door of the four-door pickup, he sighed and jumped in, curling up on the back seat while Jake positioned the crate.

On the return drive, the ability for small talk had left the space and only the burden of silence remained. "The painting..." Lily began.

"I want to see if it's really a Pissarro before we do anything," Jake replied.

"No. Not the Pissarro. Your painting."

Jake stared at the road as he drove, slowing a bit as he thought.

Lily looked over at him in profile. "You still have it."

Jake's eyes stayed on the road. "I still have a lot of things. I've also lost a lot of things."

"Lost or just misplaced?"

Jake looked over at her and then back to the road as the silence lingered. "Some lost. Some misplaced. Some thrown away." The last few minutes passed without speaking as they rattled over the stone-paved road to the parking garage of the Ann Street Wharf Condominiums. "Here," Jake said as he pulled into a slot near the garage entrance. Lily grabbed the crate as Jake opened the back door for Bromo, who immediately stepped out to the sidewalk, sniffed and lifted his leg on a favorite spot. As they turned for the door to enter the building, Lily saw the red Vespa with black trim locked in place next to Jake's truck, and was surprised at the mix of sadness and happiness that washed over her, for this day and for days before. She looked at Jake, with a sad smile that he reflected momentarily before tapping his electronic fob to open the door of the building.

Jake unlocked his condo door on the third floor, and both Lily and Bromo entered. Bromo went to a corner dog mattress and sat, staring at the two as Lily set the crate on a heavy table, made of an old ship hatch cover and positioned along one wall. Jake turned and clicked on a desktop computer. The one large room blended from small kitchen area to small eating area to small living area. To the left an open door offered a view another room and bath. To the right, stairs led up to a narrow hallway and closed door. One side wall was solid brick, and the far wall looked out over a harbor marina. Furniture was sparse and decorations absent but for a few framed photographs and a nicely rendered painting of the Domino Sugars sign that shown over the harbor at night. The wall opposite the bricks displayed several photographs of the building they occupied – some quite old. The brick wall was lined with three standing bookcases – not matching but packed with books and file folders.

"A minute while the computer boots," Jake said. "Want anything to drink? Coffee, water, beer?"

"Nothing," Lily said as she walked over and looked out the window to the harbor. She bent to scratch Bromo behind the ears, who closed his eyes and leaned into the scratch with appreciation. "Very nice place. Is the brick wall original?"

"This building used to be a tobacco warehouse, which might explain the freight rails still embedded in the street on the front side and the dock on the back. The building was never up to code, however. It burned in the late 60s. The first photo on the wall there shows the original warehouse and the second shows the building after the fire."

"Not much left," Lily said.

"Just some of the shell. Anyway, after lying in rubble for a decade, it was finally re-built as condos. That brick wall was one of the original interior walls. This was one of the first condo buildings here at the Point, in fact. In the 80s you couldn't give these units away, but in the last few years, this has all become very chic. Flop houses became restaurants and bars became taverns. I bought in when I got back to the states, just before the prices went through the roof. Probably couldn't afford it now." Jake reached into the refrigerator for a bottle of Balt Ale and poured two glasses. Lily started to object, but Jake waved her off. "We have work to do." He turned to the computer and handed a screwdriver to Lily, who immediately began to pry the crate open once again.

"How do you want to do this?" she began, sipping the beer and looking at the painting. The FBI has a protocol."

"Okay, but let's start with the checklist. The one Hoving created for the Met to screen new acquisitions, remember? It's basic and it doesn't require anything I don't already have here. Let's run it."

Lily nodded as Jake opened a desk drawer and handed her a large magnifying glass, a picture stand, and an LED light wand. She pulled a chair over to the table and sat in front of the painting, reciting from the familiar procedure. "Okay, signature. Signed lower left, 'c. Pissarro. 1873' small 'c' capital 'p' loop at the top of the 'p' double 'ss' drags below the line." She looked over Jake's shoulder to the image of a painting he had pulled up and magnified, focusing on the signature. "Yes, looks good."

"Brush strokes?" Jake said.

Lily peered through the magnifying glass, scanning the painting and looking back at the sample Pissarro painting on the computer. "Width and edging look good."

"Color pallet?"

"Hard to tell."

Jake leaned over and weaved as he examined the painting. "I agree. Nothing disqualifying."

"Smell?" Jake looked to Lily. "You take this one. You always had the better nose."

Lily smiled. "No odor of baking or pigment or fixture or craquelling solution," Lily replied, remembering the forgeries that could be detected by a faint odors, especially when it came to the chemical washes often used to duplicate the cracking of aged oil paint.

"Let's try the light." Jake said, plugging in the light wand.

Holding the wand behind the painting, they both looked intently. Jake shook his head. "I don't see any pattern in the cracks to indicate they were artificially added, by folding or pressing the canvas."

"I agree, but there is no indication of earlier works painted over. That seems odd," Lily noted, aware of how often early Impressionist painters painted over old canvases rather than spend for new ones.

Jake leaned back in his chair. "Not odd, really. If the date is listed as 1873, Pissarro was older than the other Impressionists, and he would have been successful enough by the 1870s that he wouldn't need to re-use his canvases."

Lily turned her head as she looked through the magnifying glass at the back-lit painting. She squinted, noticing where something might have been painted over. "Jake, is this a pentimento?"

Jake jerked erect and leaned closely. The presence of a pentimento, or paint-over, would strongly indicate an original work. "Art copiers don't usually change their minds. However, a smart forger might add that intentionally. And Luc was smart that way..."

Lily turned to Jake. "Can we I.D?"

Jake moved to his computer. "I'll log in to the Catalogues Raisonnes from the International Foundation for Art Research. IFAR is about as complete as they come." He typed a login name and password, and searched under Pissarro, 1873. They both looked at the images. "Of course," Jake said. "I knew it looked familiar. Here. *Gelee blanche*, the *Hoarfrost*." Jake clicked on the text data and scrolled down. "It's supposedly hanging peacefully in the D'Orsay at the moment." Jake paused and stared forward.

"What are you thinking?" Lily asked.

Jake walked over to the window overlooking the bay. It would be dark soon, and the red neon of the Domino Sugars sign would be lit, mirroring the photograph on his wall. He looked down at Bromo and then over to Lily. "I'm thinking we have to go to Paris."

Chapter 7
(Six Years Ago)

Tossing an overstuffed duffle on the floor of a small apartment tucked into the middle of the third floor of the stone and ironwork building facing Rue Cler, an old stone street in the Left Bank of Paris, Jake Daniels looked around. The key, mailed to him a week earlier, had worked smoothly in the old lock, although the adventurous ride to the third floor in the small bird-cage elevator – iron filigree groaning and rattling with every foot of ascent – revealed that it had not survived the years quite as gracefully. A window of the front room was open and the undulating murmur and clatter of the market in the street below provided an exotic and comforting background music to the afternoon - still rich with the smell of recent rain on the stone street. He pulled a small piece of baguette from a paper wrapper and took a bite, savoring the pâté and mustard inside and looking around the small space. Directly before him was a living area, surprisingly large and including an iron-framed balcony, large enough to stand out on during the expected steamy summer evenings. A door at the far end of the living space led to a bedroom, with another to his right. Directly to the right was a small kitchen area, already crowded with countertop containers, small appliances, and a large bowl of fruits and vegetables.

He had met Lucas Benoit at MICA, the Maryland Institute for the Creative Arts, almost two years earlier.

Jake had graduated from Hopkins with a degree in chemistry, and had returned to MICA at the urging of his mother - a professor of sculpture at the Institute - to explore his artistic talents. Luc was entering his last year before graduation and facing the endless task of trying to make fine art painting a means of earning a living. He had recently arrived from Lyon, France, and Jake had shown him some of his favorite haunts in Baltimore. As young and hopeful painters, they had become both friends and competitors, and had decided that aspiring artists needed to live for a time in Paris. Luc left first, as Jake was working with the conservation staff at the Walters Art Gallery, and needed to finish a few projects before he could leave. Luc had found work at an art gallery in Paris, and had contacted Jake, asking him to come and share the rent on the apartment he had located.

Jake looked into the kitchen area and tested the air with a frown. With Luc, he knew, everything would be in perfect order except the kitchen. Luc's culinary ambitions exceeded his abilities, even though he never stopped trying to master this one unconquered frontier, and he viewed cooking with the honor reserved for all things unreachable. Walking into the kitchen, Jake sniffed, walked to the sink, turned on the water, and flicked a switch to grind up whatever had been left in the disposal – however many meals ago.

In one bedroom, Jake noticed that Luc had, in the three months since he rented this apartment, already added an extra closet space. Jake remembered that several women had told Luc that he looked good in his clothes - as well as out of them. Apparently, the message had hit home. Closet space, in fact, seemed to take half of the room. Walking out and crossing to the other bedroom, he saw a brass-framed single bed – a bit fussier than he would have liked, but which looked especially inviting after the flight from BWI Thurgood Marshall airport and the crowded ride from DeGaulle on the Metro de Paris. Hauling his duffle into the bedroom and draping his jacket over the bed, Jake stretched and looked around his new room. A small desk by a courtyard window - largely blocked with an ironwork decoration and a decade's worth of unwashed glass - was pushed next to a serviceable dresser. A space in the wall next to the bed was open to a closet area, separated from the rest of the room by a heavy blue drape. The wood floor looked old, but recently sanded and refinished, highlighted by an oval carpet.

Jake stepped back to the living area and looked around the apartment once more. Like nearly everything in the 7th Arrondissement, this building was pure Old Paris style, offering homage to the Belle Epoche. Jake nodded, whispering to himself, "Perfect." Walking back into the kitchen area, he pushed up his sleeves, rummaged through the fruits and vegetables, found a few serviceable vegetables, and began to wash them. "May as well begin to earn my keep," he mumbled, whistling a Chicago blues riff as he explored cupboards and drawers.

By the time the apartment filled with the aroma of olive oil, garlic, and sautéed asparagus, Jake heard the aching metallic grind of the elevator, followed by shuffling in the hallway and a key slipping into the lock.

"Mon Dieu, you have arrived!" the voice announced as the door opened. "And this place already smells better! Now the good life begins!"

Jake turned. "Luc, how did you find this place – much less afford it?"

Luc set a clipped leather folder and small computer tablet on a low table just inside the door. "A bit of luck and a lot of searching - with the help of this amazing companion. Jake, meet Lily." With those words, a small-framed woman appeared in the doorway. Jake fought to suppress a sudden intake of breath as Lily entered the apartment, and he quickly closed his open mouth and stood upright, assuming what he hoped was a more macho pose.

"Bonjour, ravi de vous rencontrer, Lily," he said with a small nod. My God, he thought, she was beautiful. Petit, athletically slender, with auburn curly hair pulled up behind her head, eyebrows lifting playfully over amazingly dark eyes - Luc had either moved to a new league or was incredibly lucky.

"No need for French, Jake, although yours sounds quite good," she said with a laugh. "Luc has been preparing me for your arrival for the last few weeks - and it's always nice to meet a fellow ex-pat." She removed a light jacket and laid it down over Luc's briefcase.

"Lily is another American refugee. From Boston to this City of Lights - so you'll have to be careful about rooting for the Orioles if they happen to be playing the

Sox. So, Hopkins, meet Harvard. And as far as languages, don't be concerned. She speaks 5 of them." Luc sat in an armchair and Lily took what seemed a familiar place on the small sofa and nodded to the space next to her.

"So you're Jacob Daniels. Come on, time to hear all about you."

"It's Jake, and not much to tell." He wiped his hands as he sat, feeling more uncomfortable than he thought he would. "Johns Hopkins, B.A and B.S. in painting and engineering. Taking time off before grad school with some work at the Maryland Institute for Creative Arts - along with Luc --."

"His mother," Luc injected, "is a professor at MICA, so they were allowed to lower their standards and let him in."

Jake laughed, "Probably true. Anyway, Luc takes off for Paris and within a few months I hear that he's totally in over his head and needs someone to help with the finances." Jake raised his hands and shrugged. "That's about it. And you?"

Lily smiled and dismissed his question with a small shake of her head. "That's all? I already know more about you than that. But we'll let that pass for now. As for me, raised in Philly, undergrad at Harvard. Dual business and art history majors, minor in criminal justice, transfer to the Sorbonne." She also shrugged as if to end the story. "Strange that we always describe ourselves through our academics, isn't it?"

Luc filled the silence. "Yes, and with an invitation to come to Paris to help with a joining of several small art galleries into a small collective of sorts. She even helped get me a job!"

"Really?" Jake turned to Lily. "I should point out that hiring Luc shows questionable taste."

Luc walked to the kitchen area and inhaled deeply. "Lily found herself working at an art gallery that needed to find an organizational genius and top-gun researcher who also had incredible artistic talent. So of course, she got me the job! What smells so good?"

"Didn't have much to work with, but I found some peanuts and ground them up, sautéed in a bit of garlic and olive oil. Should work well with the asparagus."

"Well the place has never smelled so good." He stepped to the door. "But even the best asparagus is not a meal. I'll stop at the marché aux poissons across the street."

"Salmon would be good," Jake said from the sofa.

"Absolument," Luc said and left the apartment.

Jake and Lily both stood and moved to the kitchen. "The dishes in the right cupboard are guaranteed to be the cleanest of the lot. I washed those myself," Lily said as she walked back to the living area and cleared a few art catalogues and newspapers from the table.

"Good to know." Jake shuffled through a drawer of tableware, double-checking each but finding them all clean. Without looking away from his task, he asked, "So how long have you and Luc been together?"

"Together? As in 'working together' it's been about two months. If you mean 'Together' together, then no. We aren't."

Jake felt himself exhale and couldn't help but smile. "Okay, just asking. I guess I assumed."

Lily paused and looked over at Jake. "No time for a personal life, I'm afraid." There was a silence before she added, "Wanted to be honest, just in case you were going somewhere with that."

Jake smiled and turned to her. "I was, actually, but I hear you. Can't blame a guy for trying."

Lily looked back. She nodded and smiled – as did Jake – and they both continued their preparations.

"Merveilleux," Luc said nearly two hours later. "I'll wash dishes as my contribution to the meal." He noticed Jake's raised eyebrows and added, "and yes, I will even run the disposal this time." Before heading into the kitchen, he poured equal parts of the remaining cava into Lily's and Jake's glasses.

Jake and Lily took their wine and both sat on the couch – apparently leaving the chair for Luc. "So why did you study engineering?" Lily asked, "Isn't that a strange combination with fine arts? Were you interested in architecture?"

Jake set his wineglass on a low table in front of the couch and chair. "Don't know. Maybe I was. More likely it was just one of those things that sparks an interest, and you follow it for a while. You know how that is."

"Not really, no. I've always been pretty focused. Every step is linear movement forward, or I don't even take the step. It has served me pretty well." Lily took a sip and added, "Probably has gotten in my way also."

Jake turned on the couch to face her. "But you do know something of unanswered calls, don't you? What about the criminal justice minor? That qualifies as more or less whimsical, doesn't it? And how does that translate into an invitation to the Sorbonne?"

Lily smiled as she took another sip of wine. "Well now - that's a winding road. Next time, OK?"

Chapter 8

International air travel was a part of Jake's professional repertoire, as it was for so many others. One difference was that museums, typically non-profit institutions, rarely paid for First Class. He resented the hours folded into economy seats, despite the fact that he had learned to scratch his nose with his knees. He knew all the protocols – to leave the vent nozzle blowing to discourage the congregating of airborne vermin, to swab everything with antibacterial wipes, to get up every hour to unbend his legs and hopefully prevent blood clots, to wear a face mask...

He knew how to make the best of it.

Which made this particular flight a welcome respite. Lily informed him that his first-class ticket would be covered in her expense voucher. Once airborne, Lily reminded him that this would be a perfect time to talk about many things, but that she wanted to close her eyes for a bit first. He agreed, envious of her ability to nap on command.

Looking out the oval window into the gray foam of clouds, Jake tried to take advantage of the time to organize his thoughts.

Six years ago he had arrived in Paris excited to begin what was going to be a new adventure with an old friend, Lucas Benoit. "Adventure"? absolutely. "Exciting"? Not the way he remembered it. Terrifying, horrible, disastrous. That was more like it.

But how had *that* become *this*? There had to be a pattern, a cause/effect. Each domino pushing against the next just enough that it falls into the third, and fourth... As artists, he and Luc had both been good. No, he thought, not really as artists – more as painters. There was a difference, most likely only noticed internally, but Jake saw it in Luc, and certainly recognized it in himself. His paintings were competent – even technically perfect at times. Nevertheless, no matter how Jake tried to select subjects or scenes, his work always seemed flat. Something was always missing – something that he typically saw in others, even in those whose brush strokes were less than perfect. Like a voice produced by an algorithm – pronounced perfectly but without affect. The plane pushed through the bank of clouds and a small puddling of water formed on a corner of his window where microscopic mist had gathered. The puddle vibrated, unable to hold itself in the face of gathering mass and the physical push of nature. Finally pulling loose from its molecular inertia, it streaked across the window, leaving only a faint smear to commemorate that it had ever existed. In its fading trace, Jake remembered the many paintings he had begun or even finished – all gone now. All but one. He could even remember when the final realization struck him that he was never going to be an artist, and how that had changed the game for him. Forever, and probably much for the better. He thought also of the small orange plastic container of pills zipped into an inside compartment of his overnight bag.

But here they were, tracking the reasons for Luc's murder – or whatever that was, he thought. No, it was too much, too many dominos. There was a movement, and he turned to see Lily stir. Lily. He looked out at the clouds.

Lily.

He closed his eyes and leaned his head against the textured inner skin of the plane, rolling his head forward a bit to rest in the indentation made by the oval window. Almost immediately, an attendant offered a small pillow, which he accepted, and a blanket, which he did not. In his fading consciousness, he realized that he could get used to First Class.

The plane broke through the clouds and Jake was suddenly impaled with the burst of bright sun. Jolted awake, he turned from the window, blinked a few times to clear his eyes, and lowered the plastic shade. Whether his movements or the sudden light, Lily moved and sat upright, inhaling and exhaling heavily and turning to look at him. She smiled and he was momentarily lost in her.

"Was I out long?" she said.

"Don't really know. Dozed off myself." After a pause, he added, "I was thinking. Does Luc still have the same apartment?"

"Yes. You don't change apartments in Paris very easily."

Jake nodded. "Good. I still have a key. Let's begin there."

Lily moved her seat from its reclining position and waved to an attendant. "Some orange juice, please. Jake?"

Jake nodded.

"No. We don't begin in Luc's apartment. We begin here." She looked at him, eyebrows raised as two glasses of orange juice appeared. "First, why are you being like this? We haven't seen each other in, what, five years? I know we aren't celebrating anything. I know how messed up this is – believe me, I know. But it's been five years!"

"This isn't about us. Luc—"

"Yes, I know that too. Luc was into some deep trouble, and I'll tell you what I know if you will just – I don't know – just wake up!" Although keeping her voice low, she was breathing rapidly, and Jake fought the urge to try and quiet her. Turning, she took a long gulp of her orange juice and returned her attention to Jake, who also pausing to sip – biding a bit of time.

"Listen." Jake looked at the floor and then back to Lily. "Everything I ever knew about Luc was connected with damage." He set his glass down and turned to her again. "Yes, we were good friends. But even your best friend can bring disaster." He paused for emphasis. "Even your lover."

Lily stared, open-mouthed. "Are you serious? I never gave you anything but my love and my support! I never brought you any sort of disaster!"

"No, not you. Me. I'm the one who brought the disaster." He paused. "Brought it to both of you."

"Jake, I thought we were good together." Her voice was slower and softer, straining through long pauses as she fought for control. "I thought we fit together. I even thought we were in love."

Jake shook his head and looked away. "No. First of all, I set Luc up for trouble from the start. I knew his competitiveness, and I knew his willingness to skirt the law – and still I pushed him into that inane contest. Then, when everything went wrong, I also brought it all down on you. I knew there would be trouble and I still persisted. Luc thought I did a selfless thing when those two assholes came by, but I didn't. I was just accepting the consequences of what I had started. I put you in harm's way, and left us both with a future as mangled as my hand. I couldn't make up for doing that to you." Jake looked toward the front of the cabin. "So I left."

Lily whispered, "But you didn't have to."

"Yes I did," he said, whispering in return. "It was a cowardly move, but I couldn't stay. There would have been more coming."

Lily whispered, "You don't understand - there *was* more coming. It *did* come." As she spoke, a middle-aged balding man in the seat in front of them, wearing a blue suit tailored for "portly," turned his head slightly toward them. Jake watched as the man pretended to flip through a flight magazine. Pulling a pen from his pants pocket, Jake opened the same magazine the man was pretending to read and wrote on the margin of one page, *The guy in front of us, when did he take that seat? Wasn't it empty?*

Lily nodded and wrote, *When we slept?* Then, after a pause she took the pen and scribbled, *Nobody moves to the first row seat in the cabin, even in First Class. There is always less leg room there. I don't like it.*

Jake shook his head. *May be paranoid, but I don't like it either.*

Jake turned to her and spoke just loudly enough to be sure he was heard. "We have about half an hour before landing. I'm going to try to get another nap in. Let's just drop it."

Lily handed her empty glass to the attendant, and added, "I agree, this isn't going anywhere." She leaned back to partially close her eyes.

A short time later, the pilot announced their landing, and shortly after touching down, the airplane's cell phone indicator went green. From his sport coat pocket, the balding man pulled out a cell phone in a white case and punched in a brief text message. Jake frowned.

Lily and Jake pretended to open and examine their bags in the overhead as the man exited, not looking back and carrying only a shoulder case the size of a laptop carrier and a small soft bag. As he left the plane to the walkway tunnel, Lily let two other First Class passengers leave before following up the walkway. They watched the man pass through the custom ranks two people ahead of them and walk through the doorway to grab a quick coffee and head to the cab pickup. After a brief check, Lily and Jake walked to the large doors exiting the airport into the sun and crowds of midday Monday. From just behind the doors, they watched as the man stepped into the back seat of a silver Mercedes GLS class van pulled to the curbside.

Jake tilted his head to the side. "So why does a man in a suit travel overseas without any luggage? He certainly didn't wear one suit for his entire time in the states."

"Could he just be here for a business meeting of some sort?" Lily asked.

"Don't think so. He went through customs too quickly. I'll bet he's French, not American."

"Are you sure the painting is safe back in Baltimore? And his luggage could be delivered later," Lily added. "He looks well enough connected to have someone do that for him."

Jake nodded. "Trust me, no one will find that crate. We're the only ones who even know the wall panel is removable. And you could be right about that guy's luggage. But I don't like it."

Lily looked at the empty space where the Mercedes had pulled up and pulled away as a blue cab drove up from the taxi rank. "I don't either."

Chapter 9
(Five Years Ago)

"Get out!" Luc shouted, his voice cracking with panic. "I've already called police! Get out NOW!"

Jake turned to Lily, shouting to be heard above his friend, "Get Luc out of here! I can handle this, but get him out! You too!"

Lily turned and grabbed Luc and, despite the fact that he was still yelling at the three armed intruders, pulled him from the room. One of them left with Lily and Luc, and returned moments later. He closed and turned the lock on the doorknob. The yelling and empty threats continued, muffled behind the door.

Three men mumbled something to each other in French. They laughed at their apparent joke.

"What is it you want? I can make this right," Jake said as one of the men, holding a gun, pushed him into a wooden chair. Another man reached into a bag, and, pulling out a roll of silver duct tape, began taping Jake's legs and torso to the chair. The third man walked over and bent down to look Jake in the face.

"No. WE are going to make this right."

"This was just a mistake! That painting was never supposed to be sold. And I'm good for the money. It's a mistake, that's all this is." Jake tried to speak calmly as his left hand was taped to the chair, and his right hand brought forward and taped at the wrist to the table in front of him. "For Christ's sake, just take the money!"

The third man spoke as he reached into the bag. "This isn't about money, imbécile. Fierté. Pride. Money doesn't fix that." The man removed a flat rectangle of iron, perhaps an inch thick and 6 inches square. He also removed a hammer with a large flat head, some sort of small sledge.

Jake stared at the hammer, suddenly unable to speak. The man set the iron rectangle on top of Jake's right hand, and as Jake tried in vain to move his hand, the man lifted the hammer into the air. As the hammer swung down, all he could do was wait for it.

There was a single, guttural scream, and then there was silence. A fuse of heat shot up his arm and exploded in Jake's brain. The room seemed ablaze and he thought for a moment that his arm had been ripped from his body. A violent tremor began at his elbow and moved to his shoulder. Then Jake saw the hammer rise for a second blow, but felt nothing. His vision narrowed to a small tunnel and fell away to darkness. There may have been a third blow - or a fourth. Jake had no idea. The three men packed their bag and walked from the room, closing the door behind them and ignoring the yelling of the two tied to the stair rail. An elderly woman looked from her apartment, but when the men looked her way, she retreated and closed her door. There was a faint sound of a police siren in the distance as the three men turned right and walked down Rue Cler, into a crowd of shoppers, talking quietly together.

Chapter 10

The taxi stopped at the corner of Rue de Grenelle and Rue Cler, since Cler was a market street during the day and traffic was not allowed. As they walked the half block to Luc's apartment, Jake had to pause to separate and contain the feelings of being back at the building that had been his home for nearly a year. The street murmured with the midday Monday crowds, while Jake and Lily walked silently, Jake recalling the early morning clattering as market stands were rolled into place over the street's paving blocks. "Best alarm clock in the world," he had whispered to Lily as they stood looking out the balcony window one morning after she had spent the night. This day they had spoken little in the cab, suddenly aware that some secrecy was needed, and feeling that light touch of paranoia from the flight, which whined like a mosquito in the back of their minds. As they entered the building and rode smoothly in the old birdcage, Jake tried to open with a lighter comment. "At least they fixed the elevator."

Stepping out in front of the apartment door, Lily put her index finger to her pursed lips. Jake nodded silently. Lily removed her cell phone and held it up for Jake to see as she shut it down. Jake followed suit with his phone. Then Lily unzipped a side pocket in her shoulder bag and removed a device the size of a cigarette pack. She poked on a small antenna, pulling it about 4 inches from the device, and motioned to Jake to unlock the door. Jake looked at her and nodded to the device, then looked into the apartment. They both froze, and Lily held her hand in front of Jake to stop him while she leaned in and moved the device slowly to the left and the right. The apartment appeared as a giant snow-globe, shaken and left to roll on its side. They stepped in, and Jake stood in the once familiar living area, trying to draw the connecting line between the quiet and comfort of his memory and the apocalyptic image before him. The sofa in the living area was tipped over, it's legs in the air like a roadside carcass, material cut and stripped from the bottom. The floor was covered with scraps of paper, furniture stuffing, and bits of broken glass and china. Silently, her finger again to her lips, Lily stepped carefully around the wreckage, poking the small device into corners, around overturned lamps and tables, into closets, and carefully around the shelves and drawers of the kitchen – choosing her footing carefully to avoid the contents of drawers opened and emptied onto the floor. After a few minutes of exploration, she returned to Jake, who stood open-mouthed with his arms outstretched in silent questioning.

"We can talk," she said with a tired resignation. Then she held up the small device. "Electronic field detector. Standard issue from the Bureau. Nothing exotic. You can buy them on Amazon, if you like." She looked at Jake, who stood motionless. "It picks up active electronic signals, which is why I had us turn off our cell phones. I found Luc's router, but no microphones or cameras, so we should be fine here." Jake still hadn't moved, and his mouth was still open.

Lily looked around. "I'm guessing we weren't the first to stop by." She looked around again. "This is not good."

Jake shook his head in disbelief and looked around the apartment. "Well somebody was looking for something – and from the look of things, they were pretty frustrated about it. You didn't pick up a computer signal? Luc used both a laptop and a tablet, as I remember."

"If they found what they were looking for, there wouldn't be this much mess. And, no. I found nothing. If his devices are turned off, however, there wouldn't be any signal."

"Luc could be pretty paranoid, and he would have backed up any information he had on what was going on. That is, if he had any information." Jake paused. "Hell, we don't really even know what we're looking for, or even if there is anything to find."

"I think we can be sure there is something to find, or this place wouldn't have been trashed," Lily said, poking at a pile of books with her foot.

"Did Luc have his laptop in Baltimore? We should have looked."

"I did. Nothing was in his hotel room. His bags were still there, but there wasn't anything. The Baltimore police have the bags now, but I checked before they got there."

Jake considered what Lily had just said, as well as what she revealed without saying, and nodded. "Good to know, I guess." Jake tilted his head and looked directly at Lily. "So how much aren't you telling me, and when do I get to play along?"

"You don't understand, Jake. There are rules I have to go by."

"Really?" he replied, his voice raised. "We left the scene of a crime you were investigating without telling anyone, we are here illegally searching the apartment of a homicide victim – which also seems to be the scene of a crime – and we have knowingly hidden away a pretty significant piece of evidence. Add to that the fact that I, likely a suspect, have left the country. Are you seriously going to quote a rule book to me?"

Lily frowned and looked at the floor. "There are some things you aren't going to like, Jake."

"A day ago we stood together to identify Luc's body. I think we have gone beyond things I'm not going to like."

Lily paused and exhaled. "Okay. Let's finish up and get out of here. Then back to my place and I'll tell you everything I know. Everything."

Jake nodded and looked around the central living area. "So we're looking for papers, notes, laptop, tablet... Anything else?"

Lily shook her head. "I don't know, but we have to poke around."

They began in the living area, wordlessly shoving aside drawers and trash, riffling through the pile of books near the bookcase along one wall and peering behind it -- under sofa cushions, inverting to shake loose the pages of magazines -- and then moved to the kitchen and repeated the process.

"I don't see anything," Jake began. "Although the only perishable foods in the kitchen are a few eggs and some milk in the refrigerator and two potatoes on a shelf. I think Luc finally gave up on cooking for himself." Jake turned to face Lily. "But I was thinking, didn't he ever rent the room again? If not, where did he get the money to keep the apartment? He needed me to help make payments when I came over."

Lily looked back to Jake. "He was making better money. Better than he would have made at the gallery, in fact." She paused to let the comment register, and then added, "Okay, on to the bedrooms. I'll take Luc's. You take your old room."

They moved to opposite sides of the living area and entered the two bedrooms. "Holy shit!" Jake said almost immediately. "Check this out."

Lily walked quickly to Jake's old room and perked up her head in surprise. "He turned it into an art studio! Interesting, but why does that shock you?"

"This isn't a typical art studio is why. Yes, easel, paints, brushes cans of fluids, floor coverings, sketch paper everywhere. That's all typical. But the details are anything but."

Lily turned to look at him, squinting. "How so?"

"Okay, so Luc never cooked for himself. Agreed?"

Lily nodded.

"Yet, here in this art studio, he has a few food items that are suspicious. In the bookcase and on the floor nearby, there are tins of coffee, tea, and chicory. Luc liked coffee, but only high-end stuff, not this," he said, holding a jar of instant coffee power. "And I doubt he ever drank chicory. No, these are for tinting. He can adjust the tint of paper to make it appear aged with incredible sophistication with these ingredients." He pointed to another container on the floor. "And this tin of breadcrumbs? They can soften the darkness of chalk to simulate an old-fashioned rubbed look. And the bottle of olive oil? Really? In the art studio? No, the olive oil is used for staining the back of a canvas, just as it appears after a hundred years or so. Here's a box of gelatin for sizing. Not as easy to use as today's sizing compounds, but much more authentic if you are forging something older." Turning to face the kitchen, Jake added, "And now the eggs make sense, for egg tempera, and milk as a fixative for pencil and chalk. The potato is used to rub the canvas after it is stained with the olive oil, allowing the canvas to accept the paint." He waved his arms around the circumference of the room and announced. "This, Lily, was Luc's forgery studio."

Lily looked around, and could only whisper, "Damn."

"But where are the papers?" Jake asked. "Luc wasn't interested in any paper trail, I'm sure – but there should be something here. Have you noticed that there are absolutely no documents anywhere? Everybody has documents for something. How do you pay taxes? How do you check your credit card bills? What happened here?"

"You're right, and there are a few papers in his bedroom, but not enough," Lily replied. She turned back through the living area. "Let's check his bedroom more thoroughly."

A half hour later they stood back in the living area, a small pile of papers on the small table that they had righted and set in the middle of the room. Included was a Stokstad art history text placed in the pile because of the extensive notes written in the margins. Silence washed over them as they tried to consider what might have happened.

"We have to figure this out, and I'm too tired and too hungry to think," Jake said, leafing through the few pages they were able to recover. "We haven't eaten since - well - when?"

"Not sure, but you're right. Let's walk over to Le Pan de Michelle – it's a very quiet café just across the street – and there are tables inside." Lily gathered the papers and tucked them into her shoulder bag. "Leave our overnight bags here for now."

They walked to the door, looking back before closing the door and pushing the button for the elevator.

An hour later, still tired but at least refreshed, Jake looked again over the papers. "So this is the usual chaff: notes to call, errands and lists, not sure there is anything here that would be helpful. There are two hotel room receipts that we should check out - especially since one of them is here in Paris. Why would he stay in a hotel in his own city?"

Lily nodded, placing her napkin next to a now empty plate. "You're right, he wouldn't. There is this one sheet of loose-leaf. It's just a bunch of numbers, not in any order or with any notation. Probably means something, but I can't for the life of me think what. It's not much. I guess whoever broke in didn't go away completely empty handed."

"More secrets?" Jake rocked onto the back legs of the cafe chair. "Still?"

"What? What are you talking about?"

"You were following Luc, you said. And yet you don't know why he spent the night in a Paris hotel?" Jake rocked forward onto all four legs. "Really?"

Lily shook her head and packed the papers back into her bag. She left a few bills at the table and stood. "Let's get our stuff and go to my place."

As they rose and walked from the café lost in thought, they didn't notice an off-white Renault pulling away from the curb at the corner of the street and moving slowly into the sparse mid-day traffic.

Walking back to the apartment in thoughtful silence, they retrieved their small carry-on bags. As they turned to leave, Jake tilted his head and looked back at his former bedroom. "Just struck me what's missing. If you have become an art forger, you need lots of stuff – some of which is here. Even the brushes have to be old, probably purchased from an online collector. In fact, you need more stuff than if you were a legitimate painter, since you never know what you will be expected to forge – what time period, what materials. And you can't go shopping when an assignment comes – that takes too much time. You have to stockpile everything. But mostly you need canvas and wooden panels. You have to paint on something! So where are they? Where are the canvases – partially finished or being treated for future work?"

"What are you thinking?"

"I'm thinking he must have had another place – another studio. This place was for experimentation with chemicals and processes. There has to be someplace else."

Lily shrugged and sighed. "Another question for which we have absolutely no information," and they turned to lock the door once more.

Back on Rue Cler, Jake stopped suddenly. "Did you see a can of lentils anywhere in the kitchen?"

"Hm? No, I don't think so. Are lentils also used to create forgeries?"

Jake grinned. "Hold on one moment. I have to check something." He turned and walked back to the elevator.

A minute later the elevator deposited him back on the ground floor. Jake walked to the street, held up a can of lentils, unzipped his bag and tucked them in. "Our first break!" he said softly, still grinning. "I'm betting Luc's car is still parked in the garage on Rue Valadon, and I'm betting he still keeps a spare key on the top of the cement rafter over the car three spots to his left in the garage. A man of strange but predictable habits. Let's go."

Lily didn't move. "What about the lentils? A can of lentils?"

Jake looked over and raised his eyebrows in fake surprise. "I'll let you know at your place."

Chapter 11

Finding Luc's car in the garage on Valadon and locating the key, Lily climbed in and motioned Jake to the passenger seat, carrying two light bags from their flight, a small duffle and a handful of papers from Luc's apartment, and the can of lentils. Dusk was spreading long shadows and traffic was ebbing from its late afternoon crunch. As they turned from Rue de Grenelle onto de la Bourdonnais, Jake looked out the window to take in the last flicks of shadow and light under the trees along the avenue. The corner cafes were beginning to draw sidewalk crowds and growing rows of Vespas and Tourino mopeds were stacking in the available parking spaces. A few joggers passed the people gathering for dinner or a glass of wine with friends. He exhaled, blowing out memories and turned to Lily, looking to tell her how much he missed Paris. The car window was open a few inches, and the breeze caught her auburn hair, pulling strands in long twists behind her head. He paused, unable to speak, memories wrapped tightly around him - whether to squeeze life out of him or into him he couldn't tell. He looked down, then turned to look ahead. "Where to?"

"I have a place in the Thirteenth. At the corner of Avenue de Choisy and Toussaint-Feron. The street is nicely private." She looked over to Jake. "What's with the can of lentils?"

Jake hefted the can and smiled. "We found this can at a flea-market type stall along the river just after I moved in. I'd almost forgotten." He turned the can in his hands and gripped over the top.

"Forgot what?"

"This." Jake pulled at the bottom rim of the can, at first with no effect. Then, peripherally, Lily saw the rim loosen. Jake pulled again and the bottom rim came off in his hand. "Fake bottom," he announced, pulling a steel key from the lid. "Luc hid his post office key in here. We thought it was funny." Jake paused. "But the fact that the key is still here tells me that this is no longer just for laughs." After another pause, he turned the can upside down and squinted. "He's written the word "collector" with a sharpie on the bottom of the can – I mean the real bottom, not the fake bottom." He turned to Lily. "Does the poste on Rue Vaugirard open at nine tomorrow?"

"Nine thirty." Lily paused, glancing in the rear-view mirror. "But I think we have a more immediate problem." She nodded her head to the rear, as Jake pulled down the passenger visor, which included a mirror insert, and saw the off-white Renault behind them. "I just went around a block, a pointless move. He stayed with us throughout."

Jake paused to consider. "Okay, then, on the way to your place where will we find the most traffic lights?"

"Montparnasse, I think."

"Go that way. Adjust your speed so that you have to run a yellow. Then, once through the intersection, hit the brake. But not hard. I want a bump, not a crash."

Lily paused, her brow furrowed, then smiled as Jake pulled his phone from his pocket. She turned onto Boulevard du Montparnasse as he shuffled through the apps on his phone screen.

The Renault followed the turn, and within a minute, Lily had her opportunity. She rushed a yellow light, leaving just enough time for the Renault to accelerate and follow – but not enough time for it to stop when, not more than 20 feet beyond the intersection, she hit the brake. She eased off the brake a bit to better finesse the maneuver, and heard the welcome sound of a bump in the rear. Both cars pulled to the side. A few pedestrians slowed as they walked by, but such bumps were so common they attracted little attention.

Lily hopped out with perfect exasperation. When the driver of the Renault stepped out they spoke briefly in French, although the other driver didn't seem to want to say much. Lily asked if he was insured, and instructed Jake to step out and call their insurance. He stepped in front of the cars and held his phone in front of his face, speaking calmly.

A moment later, Lily walked to the rear of the car and gestured that there was no real damage. "Just a bump," she announced. Waving off the other driver, who was speaking on a white cell phone, she told him not to bother. Jake shrugged, pretended to say something in closing on his phone, and everyone returned to their cars. Lily drove on, and the Renault made the next turn onto Rue Campagne.

Jake turned to Lily and grinned. "You are a pro. Must be that FBI training. And I think our visitor will go and hide for a while."

"Did you get the picture?" Lily asked, feeling oddly breathless, and smiling widely as she pulled from the curb and drove on.

Jake nodded. "Several, actually."

A few minutes later, Lily entered a traffic circle, moved three-quarters around the loop, and turned onto Avenue Choisy. Two more blocks and she adeptly maneuvered a tight U-turn and paralleled the car alongside a public park. A gravel walkway meandered among the clusters of flowers and small bushes organized into a traditional formal garden pattern and leading to a central pond. A couple walked along the path while a young boy and girl played with model boats in the water. An accompanying adult was gathering blankets and toys, clearing off one of the benches facing the pond as they prepared to head for home. A row of blue rental bikes lined the park a few spaces in front of where Lily had stopped. A line of business offices and storefronts lined the opposite street. Now nearly seven in the evening, the businesses appeared closed. Several stores remained open however – just turning on evening lighting. A patisserie, and a brasserie were lit, while an interiors shop was darkened, all sharing a long faded red awning which had been rolled back. A small cafe at the end of the block sported a few sidewalk tables, only one of which was currently occupied by two young men leaning toward each other and smiling in pleasant conversation.

Single doorways were interspersed among the stores, and, gathering their bags and papers, Lily led the way to a dark brown oak door next to the brasserie. It's metal corner braces and trim gave a nearly medieval air to the massive wooden door, and offered contrast to the small gray key pad attached at waist level to the once-white stucco wall. Jake watched as Lily punched in a code, the door clicked and they entered at the end of a wide hallway leading to a rear elevator. The hallway and stairs were carpeted in a deep brown rug, patterned with beige trim along the edges. The walls were a spotless off-white, reflecting the wall lighting with a shine indicating either recent re-painting or thorough cleaning. Lily led the way and they climbed to a second-floor apartment. Again, she stopped, checked her field detector at the door, and entered another key pad code. Again, watching over her shoulder, Jake smiled as they stepped inside. Lily scanned once more – although not with the care she had used in Luc's apartment. "I have window and door sensors that alert the Bureau if there is an unauthorized entry, but I do a quick sweep just the same."

The door opened to a long, narrow living area, ending in a floor-length window overlooking the park. Walls were painted an off-white, just enough off to soften any glare yet still provide an openness and give an illusion of greater size. The floor was finished light wood, with a large oval area rug in front of a sofa and a smaller circular rug in front of the window at the far end. Both area rugs were gray and white specked, salt-and-pepper style, and contrasted with the wood-brown and leaf-green pattern of the sofa. Bookshelves of a light ash accented the light wood frames of several paintings and a photograph. The bookshelves filled one wall, angling down under the eave of a stairwell. An upper floor bedroom loft was open, with a simple white rail where it overlooked the living area. A modern metal floor lamp aimed a cone of light toward the ceiling, while a second lamp - more old-fashioned in blue and white decorative ceramic, was perched on a small end table next to the sofa. A long oval coffee table in front of the sofa matched wood color and finish with the trim of the sofa's feet and arm rests. The over-all look impressed Jake as a perfect reflection of Lily - neither fussy nor frilly, and reflecting contemporary elegance. Lily put her bag and the papers she had collected from Luc's apartment on the coffee table as Jake added the art history text to the pile and wandered to look briefly at Lily's books. They were a mix of art history, gallery catalogues, and European and American histories, although Jake also spotted a few books on neuroscience and philosophy. The larger bottom shelf was reserved for massive art collections of the sort that used to be the signature of Abrams Publishing.

As Jake put his carry-on bag on the floor by the door and set a few more papers on the table with Lily's, he looked at the paintings on the walls. A nice impressionist print and a beautifully textured black-and-white photograph of the stalls along the Seine were hung amid several original pastels and chalk sketches. Jake wondered if Lily had been working on her own skills, or if she had become close to someone artistic. The idea came with a primal anger, which Jake recognized immediately as an unfounded and undeserved jealousy, and which he also immediately pushed behind the door in his head that needed to remain closed. Lily had hung the window with a light fabric, letting in the last glow of evening light. Through the fabric, Jake could make out a low, wrought-iron window grate enclosing a small space on the outside of the recessed window. The space was just wide enough for two large pots, which he could see sprouted small fern-like plants. However, before settling in, she walked to the window to pull across heavy light-proof curtains. Only then did she switch on the floor lamp, return to the door and flick a switch on the wall which lit the entire apartment from recessed ceiling lights. The sofa faced the wall opposite the bookcase and stairway, giving view into a kitchen and eating area. Farther down and by the window was a dark wooden writing desk – an antique with a fold-down writing space, occupied by an open lap-top. Without speaking, Lily walked to the kitchen as Jake watched, pulled two glasses from a shelf and two Kronenberg beers from the refrigerator. Also silent, Jake accepted his bottle and glass and walked back to the living area. They both sat on the sofa and looked at the small pile from Luc's place. Jake found himself unable to look away from Lily, and after an extended silence, she looked back at him.

"What now?" she said, almost a whisper.

"I was going to ask *you*."

Lily looked down at the papers on the table, then looked up. Her eyes suddenly reflecting a renewed focus. "Okay." She shifted her position, pulling one leg under her on the sofa. "First the guy tailing us. Clearly, someone knows we're here, and knows where Luc's apartment was located. Likely the same person who trashed it."

"Persons - plural," Jake said, sitting back on the sofa and looking at the pile of papers. "That guy was calling somebody. Just like the guy on the plane was calling somebody."

Lily turned to Jake. "But everybody is always calling someone. Look at any crowd. The two may be connected, but we can't just assume that."

Jake shook his head. "Yes we can. Think of the phones. Two cell phones in white cases. You can buy any kind of case for a cell phone - any design, any color. Guess which color is the chosen the least?"

"White? Really?"

"Yep. Most people don't like it. Maybe it's because their phones become more invisible in white - harder to find quickly. I don't know why. But white is definitely the least sold color - and especially among men." Jake paused and looked at her again, "I'm a fount of useless trivia."

"Not so useless," Lily said. "Since it's unlikely that two men would both buy white phone cases, it must be that they were provided by some third party." They both paused. Lily pulled her hand through her hair, shaking her head.

"Don't forget the person – or persons – who killed Luc in Baltimore. He's not likely to be either of these two people. So that's at least three."

"And someone giving orders - so at least four."

"Let's figure that's just for starters." Jake exhaled heavily. "Shit, Luc, what were you into?" he mumbled.

"On another topic, Jake. About tonight."

"Not a problem. I saw a hotel about a block down the street. "I'll head over there and we can meet tomorrow morning to—"

"No." Lily stood and moved to the other side of the table. "You stay here."

"No offense, but no. We finish for the night and I'm off."

"Jake, I'm not looking to re-connect," she paused and added, "That's over. But this place is secure – and that hotel isn't likely to be. People know we're here."

"I'll take my chances."

Lily's voice rose. "'Take your chances?' What are you talking about? These people are serious – deadly serious, and we don't know who they are. They get to you and that's it!" She paused, lowering her voice to a quiet command. "And by the way, what happened to that concern for my safety? You are really going to leave? No, you stay here tonight." She stood, waiting for an argument that she would not accept.

Jake felt the door in his mind open, releasing a mix of anger, stubbornness, and over-arching respect. There was a wash of shame as her words cut into him.

It had been a self-centered comment, and he regretted it deeply. Mixing in was the growing regret that he hadn't yet told Lily what he realized about Luc back in Baltimore. Or thought he realized - after all, he could be wrong. He pushed the door in his mind closed again and fought to slow his breathing. "Okay. Got it." After a silence, he added, "Let's get to work. What does all this mean?"

Nearly three hours later, Jake pushed back from the table and rubbed his eyes, "What time is it? We have read everything on this table at least twice – compared, re-sorted, and gone through it over and over. I've got nothing. A doctor's office receipt, a few lists of art supplies – typical stuff. Some sketches and a brochure from the traveling exhibit that included the Pissaro. Probably the opportunity for stealing it. Notes in the margins of the Stockstad text are pretty cryptic - some connected to underlined passages and some seemingly unrelated. We should consider that still un-mined territory and get back to it. The other papers don't seem to mean anything. I still have no idea what's going on. You?"

Lily had followed her Kronenberg with an herbal tea, which she now sipped as she shook her head. "Nothing seems to connect to anything else. It's just random notes."

"And numbers," Jake added, rubbing the back of his neck. "Don't forget the page of numbers."

"Right," Lily sighed. "Whatever that means – if it means anything. And what does 'collector' have to do with this? I guess whoever trashed the apartment took most of the papers, probably just grabbed everything he saw. Okay," she said standing and walking to the passageway to the kitchen, "what do we know? We know Luc used a laptop."

"And a tablet."

"Yes, and the laptop was not in his luggage in Baltimore, and was not in his apartment. And neither was the tablet."

"So whoever broke into this apartment was looking for something. Either they didn't find it, or they did and trashed the place anyway."

Lily raised a finger. "Or both."

Jake started to ask a question, but noticed that she was not looking at him, but into a space over his head and far away.

"What if they found the laptop – which would have been easy to find, assuming it is connected to the router. They could probably trace the electronic signal from there."

"Then why take the time to trash the place?"

"Because they didn't find the tablet." Lily looked directly at Jake. "Whoever he was involved with must have known there was something else to find – maybe his tablet. And were frantic to get it."

"But they couldn't find it?"

"They couldn't find it." Lily sat next to Jake on the sofa. "Which means it's still 'out there' someplace." She paused and added, "assuming that's what they were looking for"

They both stared ahead silently until Jake said, "It's got to be in the apartment."

"Got to be," Lily added. "And if the tablet was off, they wouldn't have picked up its electronic signal with a sweep."

"Or it's in the theoretical second studio. Shit, we have to go back and check." Jake stood and stretched.

"Hold on," Lily said, shaking her head. "Not tonight. We don't know who's watching the place – or this place, for that matter. No, we can't go back tonight. We need to try again tomorrow."

Jake nodded slowly. "Right. First the poste on Vaugirard, then back to the apartment. The market stalls will be open then, so there won't be any car traffic." Jake paused and wiped his face with both hands. "Until then, let's get some sleep – my head is shot."

"Yes. Absolutely."

"I'll take the sofa."

"Yes. Absolutely."

Chapter 12

Luc grinned as he and Jake both worked at their easels, each putting the final touches to the week's assignment - something in the style of Monet, but using acrylics rather than oils. Lily had both of her hands on Jake's shoulders, and he felt her warmth radiate through him – shoulders to arms and through his chest to his groin – pulsing in shallow waves that marked time with his heart and his breathing. He looked to his left shoulder and could see the small curl of her fingers, slender and warm. He looked up to see Luc smiling in their direction, nodding approval of something unspoken. "The face," he said, still smiling at the couple. Jake looked up to see Lily over him, and was startled by her open mouth and wide eyes reflecting horror. He looked over to see Luc at his easel. His brushstrokes from a confident arm connected to a lean torso connected to a face – or what should have been a face but which now appeared discolored, bloated, melted into putty.

Jake tried to reach for what had once been his friend's face, but could no longer move his hand, which was nailed to the table with two long spikes. He longed to call out for help, but choked on his words. With a blinding flash of light, the force of Jake's gasping intake of breath shot him upright, coughing.

His sleep had been long in coming and short in duration, ending with the horror of his unconscious. Noticing a light in the kitchen, he walked in to see Lily sitting at a round, wrought iron table, its top covered by a stenciled print of light and dark blues - much like a close-up of an impressionist sky. Jake had thrown on yesterday's clothes in anticipation of a shower and noticed that she seemed to have done the same. She looked up from the rim of a large coffee cup, noticing for a moment his disorientation, and motioned with her head to the counter, where Jake saw a second mug and a fresh pot of coffee. The slightly burnt aroma of a good French roast was welcome, and he took the cup, poured, his right hand trembling slightly, and joined her at the table.

"Lousy night?" she asked, still peering from over her cup, which she seemed to enjoy inhaling as well as sipping.

"Better than nothing," he replied. "But not much better."

Lily looked intensely at Jake. "Me too. We have been on the move ever since this began. The discovery, the ID, the last-minute flight, the rush through Luc's apartment, and here." She paused to sip coffee. "Then, last night we finally stopped. I curled up in bed and the whole thing rushed forward, events and memories gathering all around us. We shove them to the back, and then we stop – like slamming on the brakes and everything spills forward." Lily paused again and began to cry silently. "That was Luc there in the morgue. That was Luc's apartment." She shook her head. "Luc."

Jake's chest tightened as he continued to struggle to breathe smoothly. He reached over and placed his hand on hers, and it felt warm from the coffee mug and trembled for a moment as he touched her. *I could comfort her, he thought, with one sentence - just a phrase in fact. But I can't. Not yet. I have to be sure of more.* He noticed that she began to move her other hand to rest on top of his, but then pulled it back. He could feel her withdrawal as much as see it. "I don't know what to say." He fought to regain himself and maintain the lie he had been holding from her – still not quite sure why.

Lily rocked her head slowly to the side away from him. "What to say Jake? Really? I'm not looking for you to say anything." The response was distant, not angry. She shook her head with some internal struggle – which was now suddenly resolved, and she pushed her coffee cup to the side, taking a deep breath. "You can't solve this – fix this – say just the right thing to make it okay."

Not completely. But partly. Yes I could.

She took another deep breath and did not look up. "We need a plan for today, and we need to move as quickly as we can."

Jake pushed back his sense of defeat. "Of course. What are you thinking?"

"I'm thinking it's now Tuesday morning in Paris. That means it's six hours earlier in Baltimore. By eight tonight, it will be two o'clock in Baltimore, and I will officially be AWOL."

There was silence as Lily looked up and then down again at the table top. "What does that mean?" Jake asked.

"It means that I either need to call in and explain my progress in the investigation so far, or else not call in and set off a series of alarm bells. Those bells will go off at Interpol in Lyon, but will quickly resonate over at the American Embassy near Place de la Concorde." She turned her eyes to Jake. "I reported in just after ID-ing Luc's body. They don't know about the Pissarro, and they think I'm wrapping up loose ends. So, by eight tonight, either we give up any idea of proceeding on our own and I work on damage control with the Bureau, or else I find some way to bring the FBI in on this all the way.

Jake looked up, his head tilted. "So the FBI doesn't know about the Pissarro? Then what do they think you're doing? Sorry, but that doesn't sound right. When are you going to tell me what you haven't told me yet?

Lily looked directly at Jake, unblinking. "Just drop it. Okay?"

Jake exhaled. "So we have today?"

Lily stood and carried her cup to the sink. "We have today." She turned and folded her arms over her chest. "So think on it. Please. I'm going to take a shower. I want us to have a plan." She turned to walk down the short hallway, calling over her shoulder. "And it needs to be a good one."

Twenty-five minutes later, Jake emerged from the shower and pulled on fresh clothes from his bag, burying the small plastic pill bottle deep in his pocket after holding it for several seconds. Feeling a bit more clear-headed, he walked back into the kitchen, where

Lily had set out a piece of baguette and a tin of salmon spread. Jake tore off some of the bread and added a thick dab of the salmon.

"We have two places to go," Lily began. "The poste and back to Luc's apartment for the tablet - if it's there."

"Add to that a stop at d'Orsay." Jake took a bite of the baguette. "I need to see the Pissarro. I need to see if it is actually hanging there and how it looks."

"You mean whether it's a fake."

Jake nodded as he swallowed. "I sure hope it's the real thing, though."

"Not a good idea," Lily said. "The d'Orsay opens at 9:30, and since you don't have an advance ticket you'll have to wait in line. That might be quick or it might be an hour. We can't predict and we don't have time."

"Okay, but I do have credentials from my conservation work, and I have a photo ID from the IIC – the International Institute for Conservationists. That should be enough to get me in the staff entrance before regular hours. If not, I'll just skip it and meet you at the apartment. But assuming they let me in as staff, this will be the best timing – no tourists and no guards. Strictly staff and administration, and staff are notoriously lax when they think someone is coming to see a curator. I'll ask the staff door guard to point my way to the conservator's office, and he'll likely be the only person I'll see."

"I don't like it. What if the conservator meets you? What's your plan if that happens?"

"Not a problem. I'll just ask if we can set aside some time to meet while I'm in Paris." Jake paused, and added, "But that isn't very likely."

"Seems likely to me."

"Like you said, it's before opening. You know museum life." Jake smiled. "Where is everyone in the hour before the museum opens?"

Lily returned a half smile and nodded. "Meetings."

"Yes, at a meeting. Always. And when I'm told he's at a meeting, I'll look around. If I remember the layout, most of the French Impressionists are on the upper level. I'm assuming that hasn't changed. We can take a quick look at the website to find the gallery for Pissarro."

"What are you looking for?"

Jake sighed. "Okay, if Luc is really as good as he seems to be, I probably won't be able to catch him for sure without testing equipment. However, I'm hoping he didn't completely go over to the 'dark side' and that he left his safety mark."

"Safety mark?"

"When we began trying to copy museum artworks, we told each other to include a safety mark so that the piece couldn't be marketed as a forgery, but rather as a good copy - which is legal. Luc's safety mark was his initials, LB, in red or black script on the bottom corner of the canvas."

Lily tilted her head. "I don't get it. If he initialed his work, how could the museum not notice?

"It's probably very near the edge of the canvas. And if the original was taken and replaced with a copy, the mark could be hidden under the frame, or even at the edge of the fold-back of extra canvas behind the frame. No one would have looked if they weren't suspicious. You have to get behind the painting and look at where the canvas is tucked under the frame. Our copies included about a half inch of untreated canvas for clean framing. That's where I'll find it – if it's there."

Lily snapped a plastic lid on the salmon and put it in her refrigerator. "I'll drop you off at the d'Orsay and then go over to the poste. We can meet at the apartment."

"But I have the apartment key. What about you?"

"I'll take the key because you'll be walking back from the d'Orsay and I'll likely get there first. When we were there last night, we pulled closed the window curtain facing Cler. When I arrive, I'll open it. If you get there first, just wait and watch the window."

"Very Cold War," Jake began, looking to lighten Lily's serious tone, but to no effect. "Okay, sounds good. But don't drive me to the d'Orsay. If someone knows Luc's car, we should take two taxis."

"I have my own car in the garage, but you're right about being followed. You take a taxi to the d'Orsay, and walk from there to Luc's." Lily opened a kitchen drawer and pulled out two black phones. "Take this. They're single-use from the Bureau. There is no web access or any sort of app, since those can be used to locate the device. There are two numbers in the contacts. Contact A calls this," she said putting an identical phone in her jacket pocket. "Contact B is direct to the Bureau." She looked at Jake. "Don't hit that one."

"Right," Jake said, taking in the change in Lily's demeanor and pocketing the phone as they both moved to the door. "We meet at Luc's in about an hour. A quick look for the tablet and then we get the hell out."

At the entrance, Jake moved to the door while Lily turned toward the parking garage. They paused and looked at each other for a moment. The pause lingered, then "Be careful," Lily said, turning for the garage.

Chapter 13

The taxi pulled up on Rue de Lille at the rear of the grand old train station, built in 1898 and now serving as the Musee d'Orsay, and Jake walked to the staff entrance, tucked in beside a large construction trailer. Although built with the Beaux-Arts glamour of the turn of the last century, and often referred to as the most beautiful building of old Paris, the staff entrance at the rear looked much like any urban solid wall - utilitarian, gray and anonymous. Jake introduced himself to the guard, and received a sympathetic, if uninvolved, response in serviceable English. He offered his credentials as a conservation consultant with ties to several American museums, and asked to speak with the Conservateur de la Conservation. The guard nodded, focused instead on a computer screen displaying what Jake assumed to be a weekly report - and informed him that all department administrators were currently engaged in a Director's meeting, and would be for another half hour at least. Jake asked for directions to the conservation department where he would pass the time with the staff. The guard made a quick phone call, gave Jake a floor plan with the conservation office quickly circled, a temporary "staff" lanyard, and buzzed to unlock the door to the museum.

Jake walked the half flight from the staff entrance to the ground floor and was - like every time he had been here while living in Paris - frozen with wonder. He gazed up to see the massive glass arched ceiling panels - glowing the light and warmth of a Paris morning and casting lined shadows on the massive open space. The narrower galleries of the first floor opened to the wider spaces above, giving the feeling - enhanced by the absence of tourists who would soon fill the lower concourse with a reverential buzz of hushed conversations. The lower level galleries, tucked into rooms along both sides of the concourse, promised an intimacy with the works within, and enticed visitors to peek into the spaces before entering to browse. At the far end, the massive clock, incredible in the intricacy of its decoration, dominated the glass and steel panels behind it. The clock that, more than a century earlier, had helped Parisian commuters locate their trains, still kept perfect time. The station itself, however, did not segue to modern times so easily. The train platforms were much too small for newer and longer trains, and the building was converted for several alternative uses before nearly being demolished in the 1970s. Fortunately, the beauty of its architecture was the catalyst for a movement to convert it to this current home for a massive collection of Impressionist and post-Impressionist art. And yet, with all of its dramatic history, the one aspect everyone remembers foremost is the clock.

It was 9:12.

Walking to one of the stairwells, Jake promised himself that he would return when he would be able to enjoy these treasures at a pace and in a mood restored - when some sort of justice and balance had finally replaced the horror of the events of the last two days.

Maybe there would even be time for redemption, he thought – redemption for Luc, redemption for himself. On the upper level, he turned to the left and walked to Gallery 32.

On entering the gallery, he smiled at the sudden image of Monet's *Essai de Figure en Plein-air*, feeling the wind that blows her scarf and frames the green tones of the underside of her umbrella. There was Sisley, there was Morisot, and of course, there were the Pissarros. On the far wall of the gallery, he spotted his target, *Gelée Blanche.* Glancing to the left and right, he approached the work, turning to note that there was still no one in sight. Standing in front, Jake examined the brush strokes and texture, much as he and Lily had done with the version in his Baltimore apartment. Reaching for the frame, he froze - hearing footsteps behind him that suddenly halted. Trying to look casual, Jake turned to see a young woman in a deep burgundy blazer and slacks staring at him from the gallery entrance.

"Puis-je vous aider?" she said, tilting her head to the side. After a pause, she added, "May I help you?"

Jake offered his best smile. "No, thank you. I'm expected at the conservation department as soon as the department heads meeting is over."

The woman paused for a few seconds. "Wait there for a moment please." She removed a small device the size of a flip phone from a pocket in her blazer and pressed a button. "Sécurité," she said, taking her eyes off Jake for a moment to look at her device. "Sécurité," she repeated. Shaking her head and pocketing the device, her eyes noted the temporary staff lanyard Jake was wearing. "That meeting should be over soon, I expect," she said as she left. "You should meet your contact at his department, however," she added, leaving, her back already to Jake.

Jake exhaled heavily and turned back to the painting. Glancing once more over his shoulder, he pulled the bottom of the painting forward an inch. He removed from his pocket a small rectangular mirror he had borrowed from Lily's bathroom earlier and held it behind the painting. After sliding the mirror slightly to the right and left, he found it. At the edge of the raw canvas, only partially visible just over the wooden rim of the frame, were Luc's initials.

"Shit." Jake turned and walked back to the corridor, down the stairs, and exited the d'Orsay just as the clock chimed for nine thirty and the doors opened to an enthusiastic public.

It took most of the walk back to Rue Cler for Jake to organize this thoughts. When he arrived at the cafe across from Luc's apartment, he was surprised to notice that the window was still closed. He had been certain her errand to the poste would be much faster than his to the d'Orsay. He sat at a small sidewalk table back against the wall of the cafe and took Lily's phone from his pocket. A waitress walked to him, but he smiled and waved her off and she smiled and walked to another table.

Looking once more at the closed drapes of the apartment, Jake paused and then tapped the first contact on the phone.

After the sixth ring and with his pulse quickening, Jake closed the connection.

Nearly a minute later, the phone rang.

"Lily?" he asked as he accepted the call.

"Jacob. Yes, it's me."

"Things have become more complicated. We have to talk options. How close are you?"

"I'm here already, Jacob," she said flatly. "I have his tablet. Come on up and we can talk."

Jake began to stand, and just as quickly sat back down. Lily hated the name Jacob. Furthermore, there was absolutely no reason to announce that it was she on the line, as if it could have been anyone else. And, of course, forgetting their arranged signal. He looked again at the apartment window, his mind sifting through options.

Standing, he looked once more at the phone, walked across the stones of Rue Cler to the apartment building entrance, and tapped the second contact.

Chapter 14

"Agent Fallsborough," Martik said, standing to shake the hand of the young man who had just entered his office. "Thanks for stopping over to talk."

"Not a problem, detective. I came over after your inquiry into Agent O'Connell. We weren't immediately aware that she was involved in any sort of local investigation, and this gives us a chance to catch up and compare some notes, I hope." The young man pulled lightly on the crease of his slacks and sat in the chair opposite Martik's desk. He wore "the uniform" of navy suit, light blue shirt, and conservative blue tie - and he wore it well. Martik had worked with the FBI in the past and made a mental note that Fallsborough, although young, was no rookie. He carried himself with the poise and assurance of someone who had worked often with conflicting jurisdictions before - and had also covered for fellow agents when the need arose. The choice, Martik recognized, was probably carefully determined.

Martik walked to a coffee pot on a counter along one wall, otherwise stacked with papers and file folders. He poured himself a cup into a light blue Johns Hopkins mug – much in need of washing – and held the pot in offering to the visitor. He caught Fallsborough's brief glance at the sooty darkness of the pot and fought back a half smile as he shook his head and waved his hand.

"No, thanks. I'm good."

"Smart move," Martik said as he sat back at his desk. Taking a sip, he looked over his cup at the freshly showered and shaved young man. "So," he began slowly. "My first inquiry into the whereabouts of Lillian O'Connell drew a blank. Should I ask if she is on some sort of covert assignment?"

The agent shifted slightly, but maintained his professional smile. "Not at all. A mix-up of names is all. Our computer didn't bring her up under her maiden name."

Martik set his cup on the desk. "Come again."

"Agent Nichol. For some reason, gave you her maiden name: O'Connell."

There was a long pause as Martik looked down and to the left, at nothing in particular, mug poised in the air half way to his mouth. "I also gave you the name of Jacob Daniels. We have a thin sheet on Mr. Daniels, narcotics violations, but nothing else. Did his name register with you? And also," he said without looking up, "is Agent Nichol on assignment?"

"No information at all on Mr. Daniels. And yes, we can talk about Agent Nichol's assignment," Fallsborough replied with an open smile. "She was investigating an art fraud case."

"In Baltimore?"

"Not originally. Seemed to be a local French matter, but apparently her trail led here."

"A trail leading to the former Lucas Benoit?"

The agent shifted and frowned. "I'm not sure how much I can confirm about an identity, detective."

"This is now a likely Baltimore homicide, agent. I'd appreciate everything you know about it."

Fallsborough smiled. "Well I will certainly consider that, detective."

Martik looked up and tilted his head slightly as he met the agent's gaze. "Well, if you aren't here to share information, why are we talking?"

Fallsborough frowned and leaned forward, folding his hands on the edge of Martik's desk. "Detective, I'm here because we need to take the body to our office in DC." He paused unmoving, his stare directly on Martik, who returned the look and nodded slightly.

"You understand that he is scheduled for an autopsy to determine cause of death."

"Yes, and we should halt that before you begin."

There was a long silence as Martik continued to look at Fallsborough; then looking back to his desktop he leaned back in his chair. The creak of his chair echoed in the amplified silence. "So I can assume you have nothing you want to tell me?"

Fallsborough shrugged and nodded. "With my regrets, detective."

"Well then," Martik said standing. "I guess we're done for today." He extended his right hand to shake as Fallsborough stood.

"Detective," he said slowly, all pretense of friendly cooperation vanished, "what about the body?"

Martik walked around the agent and opened the door to his office. "I'll certainly consider it."

Chapter 15
(Ghent, Belgium, August 1945)

The afternoon sun did not bake Alexander Wilson so much as steam him. Summer afternoons in Belgium, of course, could be like this, and he shrugged off the discomfort. His mission, after all, was of much greater significance than his comfort. The roar of the props on the Douglas C-54 Skymaster faded as it taxied from the gate to the maintenance yard, and Wilson paused to survey the airstrip built hastily just before the conclusion of the war in Europe a few months earlier. A tall and solid figure, Wilson tried not to actually bend over to greet the older, portly man approaching with quick short steps and hand outstretched.

"Mr. Wilson, I am Colonel Briolle, recently retired and reassigned here to head the restoration project we spoke of earlier. Let me first say how grateful the people of Ghent, as well as I, are for your generosity."

Wilson shook the man's hand and shrugged off the compliment. "I'm just glad I can help out, Colonel Briolle. We defeated the Nazis on the fields and in the skies, we should continue to work together to heal the wounds they have left in our culture – particularly in the arts. I am more than proud to be here to help out." He placed a fatherly hand on the older man's shoulder as they walked to the terminal building. "And I do appreciate your fine English. My French is, I'm sad to say, atrocious."

Briolle smiled, nodded, and replied as they walked to the cinderblock building. "Yes, hopefully we can follow one great day with another. Your army's small contingent of, what you call Monument soldiers has performed a tremendous service for many grateful nations, and your offer of assistance is most welcome as we continue to re-establish our art and our history. This could be the end of a long and sad story for our wonderful altarpiece, you know. And please, call me Adain – or Monsieur if you prefer. But no more Colonel - I have had enough of military titles and am glad to set them aside."

Wilson held the door as they entered the small building. A uniformed Belgian soldier checked his passport as another soldier arrived with his two suitcases. "I gather the Nazis were not kind to the panels. How long were they hidden in the salt mine?"

"Almost a year. The salt is just a minor insult to these beautiful works, however, and the constant temperature of the mines actually helped minimize damage. The panels of the Ghent Altarpiece have been looted, damaged and repaired, lost, stolen and recovered in incidents dating back to the Reformation. Jan van Eyck, as well as many of his contemporaries, considered the altarpiece his finest achievement. In my research here, I confess that I have also been caught hold by their beauty and elegance. But such tragedy. There were many attempts to destroy them as Europe's Catholics and Protestants fought each other – both sides in the name of God, of course. This century has been no kinder. The panels were broken up and sold prior to the first War and only re-assembled as German reparations after the Armistice." The older man then sighed and shook his head slowly.

"Yes," Wilson said, "that's when my father was alerted to their story. He wanted to offer his help in their restoration, even before the Nazi advance, but he died much too young. His legacy is mine now, and I'm happy to be able to put his wealth to good cause."

"Your father's legacy, you say?" Was he also a military man?"

"Not as a career, no. My father spent the first world war in the trenches here – first in France, and then into Belgium as the Axis began to crumble. He remained Private Otis Wilson until the end, however. And after armistice, he pursued his teaching career and his growing art collection." Wilson paused to smile. "I have to say, his fortunate art purchases at the end of the war remain the core of my collection, and the catalyst for my interest in working to rebuild, in whatever small way I can, the remarkable art history of Europe."

Briolle nodded in the silence, finally adding quietly, "My sorrow for the loss of your father. And sadly the story of the sorrows of the altarpiece continues. Even in the time leading up to this war. Two panels were stolen – or perhaps lost – in 1934 – or perhaps it was 1936. The records are scattered and incomplete. Andre Peeters, who kept many of the records of the Ghent cathedral discovered that two were missing. Some records, if reliable, indicate that they were returned with the others at the end of the first war, but of this I cannot be sure. Sadly, Peeters did not survive Hitler's invasion, and we may never know the full truth."

"Yes, I had heard of the two missing panels, but finding these others was certainly an act of providence, and perhaps even the missing pieces can be located." Alex knew he sounded naively optimistic, but he felt obliged to offer some comfort. "And think of how much you have saved, after all."

Briolle looked up at his guest. "We will be happy to make good use of some of your money," he said with a smile. "Have you ever seen the panels?"

They walked to a car, with the serviceman carrying Wilson's luggage, and climbed into the rear seat. The serviceman took his place as driver. "I've seen photographs," Wilson said, "But not the real thing."

Briolle settled in the car and tapped the driver on the shoulder. "You are in for quite an experience, I guarantee you."

Forty minutes later a slow drive around roadside craters, through deep ruts, and beside burned out vehicles and artillery destroyed and left behind in a hasty German retreat concluded at a large hanger – more cinderblocks with a curved roof of corrugated iron. As they drove, Alex took in the slow but visible reclamation and rebuilding to the surrounding town. He followed his host into the hanger and was surprised to find the interior well lit, efficiently guarded and meticulously organized, and immediately realized that he had no reason to think that all of Ghent reflected the ruins that he had just seen. At a row of tables lining the left of the hanger and covered with padded cloth were a series of large wooden panels, most approximately three feet wide and perhaps five feet tall. A few more likely at least six feet in height. Most were rectangular although a few were rounded at the top.

"We are working on mitigating the salt damage and cleaning the panels, so they are not at their best for showing right now." Briolle smiled and waved generally to the tables, "But you can get an idea."

Alex walked over and looked down at the panels. He took a quick breath. "My God," he whispered, "I had no idea. I – they are – my God." His voiced trailed off as his eyes wandered over the tables.

The older man looked over the panels. "Yes, I am also at a loss for words."

Alex walked up and down, unable to take his eyes off the panels, turning his head to view each one as if from different angles. "The team I spoke to you about," he said without taking his eyes from the panels, "the conservation team from the Metropolitan Museum in New York, will be here tomorrow. They have developed special treatments for water and fire damage, varnish removal, coloration, and much more that I don't fully understand. They will help your team bring these images to life. Although," he shook his head slowly, "they already seem alive."

Alex Wilson gingerly touched one of the tallest panels, rectangular although painted with a rounded top. He knew from his research that this was the image of God upon his throne, as Jan van Eyck imagined.

This image of God was beautifully peaceful, his right hand raised in the sign of wonder and grace. The eyes, half closed, hypnotically offered peace and forgiveness – and the beautifully clear crystal of his scepter seemed to conflict with the idea that this was, in fact, just paint. Alex lightly touched the hair-thin rays of gold forming the halo of God and shivered at the touch. Varnish had dulled what he suspected was a glorious red robe; and golden crowns lay at his feet.

He looked again at the tables. He was lost in miracles.

"And the two panels missing?" he whispered.

"Yes, one panel depicts John the Baptist, and the other is one of two panels depicting the Just Judges." He pointed to a photograph of the assembled altarpiece and noted the missing pieces.

"We have to find them," Alex said, still unable to clear his throat or speak above a raspy whisper. "We can start with a reward for information. A large enough reward to persuade a thief that the money will be better than a stolen panel which can never be displayed to anyone."

"If they were actually stolen, Monsieur Wilson. To be honest, we are not sure of this."

"If the panels were stolen, we will get them back, and if they have been lost, we'll find them," Alex replied as if stating an obvious fact, once again able to make eye contact with his host.

Chapter 16

Jake pocketed the black phone, reaching into his pocket to feel the comfort of the small orange pill bottle, and walked slowly up the back stairs to Luc's apartment. The elevator suddenly seemed too noisy and claustrophobic. Everything was completely quiet, even from the two other occupied apartments on the third floor. Pausing for a moment, he pushed open the door to the stairs and looked down the hallway. Luc's door was ajar a few inches.

"Lily," he called, trying to sound casual although his voice was suddenly hoarse and his throat dry. He was not surprised that there was no answer. He had heard her voice on the phone, of course, and if she was indeed in the apartment, the safest thing for her would be for him to enter – whatever the outcome. And if she wasn't in the apartment, then, he realized, that would be even worse. There had been no immediate response after he hit the second contact on the phone – the one direct line to the FBI, and he had turned the sound off as he started up the stairs.

Walking to the door, Jake announced, "Well I hope you had better luck than I did. I didn't really learn much of any--" He stopped just inside the door, facing a tall husky man in a tight, dark blue shirt. Thick upper arms flexed inside the shirt and thick black hair had been oiled and combed back into a shape much like some sort of helmet. His eyes met Jake's and stared, unblinking. A small nod directed Jake's gaze to a thick black handgun pointed at his midsection. Instinctually, Jake slowly raised both hands to the level of his shoulders, palms facing the man. He looked back at the gunman and said nothing, unmoving until the man stepped to the side and directed Jake to enter the apartment. He then closed the door and motioned Jake to sit on the disheveled sofa, it's cushions slashed and bleeding white batting.

"What do you want?" Jake asked. When there was no answer, he added, "Where is she?"

The gunman stood unmoving and staring at Jake. After an agonizing pause, he growled, "You know what we want."

Jake paused and considered the "we" he had just heard. "Why don't you fill me in?"

The man attempted a smile, and was able to approach something of a sneer. "Cut the shit. The Collector wants his painting."

Jake paused again before responding. "So where is she?"

The gunman's shoulder's heaved in a sigh and he lifted the gun to point more directly at Jake, waiting for effect.

"Forget that," Jake said. "You haven't shot me yet, so I'm guessing you won't. Or have been told not to." A silence followed and no one moved. Finally, Jake added, "So where is she? And what or who is the Collector?"

"Look asshole, I've got a job to do here." The gunman stepped closer to Jake. "I either get information from you or I beat it out of you. Are we clear on that?"

Jake managed to fake a grin. "Look, let's cut to the chase. You aren't running whatever this is, so why not tell me where she is and maybe we can settle this." He paused once more. "Or kill me and good luck keeping your 'job'."

The gunman shrugged and reached his left hand into his jacket pocket, still holding the gun in his other. His hand emerged wrapped in a metal band. Jake watched as the man approached him, fist raised, and at some corner of consciousness wondered why he wasn't terrified – or even intimidated. Instead, he felt strangely removed, as if watching from a dreamscape bleacher seat as the action played out below between two actors, neither of which seemed to be him.

The gunman shook his head. "Christ you are an asshole." He elbowed Jake against a wall and leaned into him, one hand on the gun and the other, metal-banded, raised to come down on his face.

And the gunman's phone buzzed.

The man stepped back and reached into his jacket pocket with the hand he was about to use on Jake's face, struggling as the metal band made removing his phone awkward. His gaze dropped for a moment to his pocket and Jake stepped to the side and kneed the gunman in the groin, hitting so hard that he thought he might have dislocated his own kneecap. The man's gun dropped to the floor and as Jake scrabbled to get it, he felt a hard shoe in his stomach. Unable to inhale, he reached to slap the gun into the next room. Still grunting to take in air, Jake kicked his legs and toppled the gunman onto him. They rolled over on the floor, the gunman unable to find purchase to swing his knuckled fist.

Suddenly Jake was free and scrambled, crab-like, into the room. In the next instant, however, the man was on top of him again. Again he felt a kick in the stomach, and his vision collapsed to a tunnel, through which he could just make out the unfocused image of a man over him reaching to the floor beyond his head to grab something. Jake felt around blindly for anything he could use, finding only one of Luc's paint brushes, the hairs crusted over. He hadn't breathed since the first kick and some part of him realized that he was about to pass out and, shortly after, die either of asphyxiation or from the efforts of the gunman, who was now lying on top of him. As the gunman turned his head to the side to grab hold of the gun, Jake jammed the thin handle of the paint brush into the man's nostril. The gunman reached to grab the paintbrush, and Jake grunted and pushed the handle as hard as he could. The handle stopped, then something cracked, and then it moved in deeper, the resistance of bone now gone. Blood briefly erupted from the man's nostril, and he went slack and rolled onto the floor.

The buzzing of the gunman's phone stopped, but Jake, unconscious, never heard it.

Jake's first spasmodic intakes of air came seconds later, although he was unaware of the passage of time. The first were squeaking gasps, as if holding the neck of a balloon to let the air out in a whine. Then the squeaking faded, Jake's hand twitched, and his eyes fluttered open – still unsure of where he was. As his head cleared, he lifted himself on one elbow and pushed the body of the gunman from his legs – staring at the corpse but not yet processing what was done. What he had done.

Rising to his knees and then holding the wall to pull himself to his feet, Jake took in the scene, his body aching and his head and neck weaving slightly. Holding to the wall, he stumbled to the kitchen doorway just as the apartment door opened. Two men, one in dark suit the other wearing a pin-striped shirt and dark tie, stepped into the room and muttered something to each other in French. Jake was about to run and dive for the gun which still lay on the floor of the studio room, when he remembered hitting the second contact on Lily's phone. "FBI?" he said hoarsely.

The man in the dark suit nodded, looking over the scene in the apartment. "Are you okay, Mr. Daniels? Shall I call for an ambulance?"

Jake shook his head. "No, we need to hurry. They have an agent with them. This guy—" Jake waved in the direction of the corpse.

"Yes, Mr. Daniels," the man said with a thick accent. "We are aware. You should come with us now." Both men stood in one place at the doorway, surveying the apartment but not showing any interest in entering or looking around.

Jake stumbled in their direction. "Yes, but we can't waste time. Lily – Agent O'Connell is being held." He swallowed another gulp of air. "Don't know where."

"Yes, we know," the same man said. The other hadn't spoken at all. The first man reached for Jake's arm. "You should be relieved to know that our agent is safe, and we are currently determining our next move. Come with us now. We need to hurry and, despite your objection, I think you need some medical attention." He led Jake to the door.

Jake turned and waved to the corpse of the gunman. "But what about him?"

"Don't worry, Mr. Daniels, we'll take care of that." As they came into the hallway, the first man stopped at the elevator. "We're taking the elevator. I'll have my partner secure the apartment and take the stairs. I don't really trust three adults in this machine at the same time." He turned to the man who had been completely silent. "Verrouiller la porte et prendre les escaliers." The other man nodded and turned back to the apartment.

By the time the elevator came to a stop, the other man was already waiting. They exited, Jake leaning for support on the first man, but slowly getting his legs again.

"We have a car around the corner. Can you walk there?"

Jake nodded, took a deep breath, and straightened up to walk on his own.

A black Renault Megane was parked along the curb, rear windows entirely blacked out. Jake was relieved that the FBI had transport where he could not be seen by whomever was still lurking near the apartment. The second man pulled keys from his coat pocket and beeped the car open. Jake and the first man got in the back seat while the silent partner sat behind the wheel.

"This is pretty urgent. I have important information for Agent O'Connell that I need to deliver as soon as possible." Jake said, trying unsuccessfully to hide his anxiety.

"Yes, we know, Mr. Daniels. We'll be just a short time." the first man said.

Jake sat back to try and collect his thoughts, when he noticed the driver pulling a white cell phone from his pocket to make a call.

Chapter 17
(Ghent, Belgium, September 1945)

Adain Briolle knocked on the metal door that had been installed to separate Alex Wilson's temporary office from the rest of the hangar where the newly-arrived conservation crew from New York's Metropolitan Museum of Art had begun work on the panels. On another table adjacent to those at which the men worked was one more panel, covered with canvas. A Belgian officer, still in uniform, was seated nearby, recording notes in a deep green three-ring military binder. Opening the door half-way and seeing Alex smile at his presence, Briolle entered and reached out his right hand.

"Monsieur Wilson, my congratulations is equaled by my indebtedness to you. I cannot believe that you have found and returned our John the Baptist to us! That is remarkable!"

Alex shook the offered hand heartily and they both sat. "Nothing heroic, Adain, and I'll tell you all about it. But first, welcome back! How are conditions at St. Bavo's?"

Briolle smiled, and Wilson realized how rarely he had seen the man smile. "Conditions in Ghent are not nearly as bad as they might have been. It seems that the German retreat focused more on speed than on damage. Over the last few weeks we have actually completed many of the repairs to the cathedral. Most of those were superficial - what you would call 'cosmetic.' Fortunately, there seems to have been no serious structural damage. In fact, when your work is done here, we can explore the reinstallation of the altarpiece in its original home. An exciting prospect indeed!" Briolle paused, still smiling. "So then, Alex, tell me the story of the John the Baptist panel."

Wilson tipped his metal desk chair back, and lifted both arms in happy resignation. "I simply made the reward sum more attractive than keeping the panel forever hidden. The thief contacted me a week ago last Monday and offered to turn it in on the condition of his anonymity."

"So, we will not know who stole this?"

"That was part of the bargain, I'm afraid," Alex replied with a shrug. "The thief threatened to destroy the panel if anonymity was not part of the deal. I thought having the panel returned was worth more than his arrest."

Briolle nodded. "Of course, of course." The older man paused, and then asked, "So this thief knew nothing of the remaining panel, the Just Judges?"

Alex looked down at the papers on his desktop, and shook his head sadly. "I am sorry, Adain, but I have no news of the last panel. Furthermore, the rumors I have been able to gather have not sounded hopeful." He looked up at the man who now seemed a bit older and wearier than just a few moments before.

"What have you heard?"

Wilson paused and looked directly at Briolle. "I will be frank with you. Everything I have heard – and it is not much, I have to say – tells me that the panel was destroyed."

Briolle's shoulders slumped, and he whispered, "No."

Wilson nodded solemnly. "Yes, it does appear that way. It is most likely that the panel was in the keeping of a different thief than the one I located. They planned to meet later to decide what to do with their contraband, but the other man never showed up. It seems likely that he was about to be captured and burned the panel to save himself from prison."

"No. No. Are you quite sure?"

"This is all very chaotic, Adain, so there is no such thing as 'sure.' However, it seems as if these rumors are true."

There was a long silence as the two men considered this new reality.

After a while, Alex broke the quiet. "However, I have been thinking of a plan. A plan which I think will make the best of this tragedy."

Adain Briolle looked up.

"One of my colleagues here in Belgium is an art restorer – a Mr. Van der Veken. He has been working here with the conservation team. He is quite solitary, but I will introduce you to him. Van der Veken fashions pieces of paintings that have been damaged beyond repair. He is quite good at restoring the old masters, and has even re-painted part of a Van Eyck for a museum in London. In fact, the curator of the museum where this work is now displayed has a difficult time determining where the original work ends and the restoration begins. He has labeled the work for the public as 'restored' of course, but some of his own colleagues have a hard time believing it."

"What are you suggesting? That we include a forgery in the altarpiece?"

"Not at all Adain, and please hear me out. My colleague has photographs of the lost panel, and of course he has access to these originals, from which he can determine chemical compounds, colors and other secrets of the originals -- although he is quite familiar with the materials and techniques of Jan van Eyck . He has been working as an advisor to the conservation team. He knows how to replicate the colors, the chemical compositions, and the techniques. He will even use materials and equipment to mimic Van Eyck." He paused for comment, but Briolle remained silent. "All I'm saying is let him try. When he has finished, you can approve or disapprove of his result. We don't try to pass it off as the original, but are completely honest and label this as a replica of the lost panel."

"Monsieur Wilson, I have to say I am not sure of this. However, it may be the only way to restore the full story of the altarpiece – with all of the panels intact." He paused to consider further, as Wilson waited. "Your instincts have been correct so far, and I think the gratitude of the people of Belgium owe you the chance to follow this idea. Yes, let's go ahead with the, what do I call this, a forgery?"

Alex Wilson laughed once. "No, no, Adain. Not a forgery. Call this simply a restored panel, created with admiration for Van Eyck, the master."

Briolle nodded. He then looked up. "But what if the Just Judges panel is recovered at some point? What if it has not been destroyed? Will that create a problem? And what of this colleague of yours? Is he in agreement with this plan? How much shall we pay him for copying a work of art that is priceless?"

Wilson shook his head. "These are not problems. The man works for me. I will pay him for his efforts. And if the original turns up after all, it would be a wonderful surprise. I would then enjoy an incredible copy of the original in my home – to remind me of our time together on this project."

Briolle stood and nodded to Wilson. "Monsieur Wilson... Alex...there will come a time when art history texts will highlight our work here. I expect your name will be featured among the heroes who have worked to restore the heritage and the culture of our nation – and even of Europe itself."

Wilson also stood. "We have all done what we are able to do, Monsieur Briolle. We all have reason to be proud."

Chapter 18

The black Renault Megane had been maneuvering with relative ease through the streets of Paris, so Jake assumed most of that time was spent on the Boulevard Périphérique, the limited-access highway which ringed the city. However, the blackened glass which would prevent others from seeing into the car also prevented his seeing out – as did the dark partition that had been raised behind the front seats of the car - so even with his limited knowledge of the streets and neighborhoods surrounding the city, he had no idea of where he had gone, or where he was. He noticed that the doors did not have manual locks inside.

The man next to him watched his glance at the door, and turned to him. "I see Mr. Daniels, from your sudden silence these past several miles that you suspect we are not the FBI. Let me assure you that you are correct."

"So then what do you want? You want something."

"Very true!" the man said with what seemed a genuine laugh. "But no, we are only the messengers – the delivery service. We are taking you to a place where our employer can speak with you. It won't be long now."

"Why bother?" Jake said, not even trying to keep the anger from his voice. "You have me, you have Agent O'Connell. What do you need? Why this waste of time?"

The man turned back to face the front. "Just the delivery service. Just the delivery service."

Jake rode in silence, considering possible outcomes for Lily, and what his options might be. The man next to him didn't react or deny that they had Lily, so it seemed likely she was still alive. He still had the Pissarro, and he hadn't been killed - so it was possible they (whoever they were) realized that. It was also possible these two knew nothing about it – especially if they actually were the 'delivery service.' For the last several minutes the car had maintained a steady speed. There had been no stops or turns. That would indicate that they had moved beyond the city limits to one of the limited-access national highways. Jake tried to picture the map of highways out of the city, but had no way to tell which direction they might be headed – and with the panel up separating the rear seat from the front of the car, there was no way even to judge the position of the Sun. He assumed it to be nearly noon, although he couldn't be sure. Suddenly, he fell forward as the driver crunched the brake hard. Just as suddenly, inertia pushed him back into the seat as the car sped up. The panel behind the driver slid down a few inches, light pouring into the rear compartment.

"Nous sommes suivis," the driver said in a low voice. Jake picked up the word 'suivis' as 'followed.'

The man next to Jake reached over to the front and pushed a button which lowered his window. Jake noticed the sun high in the sky, but visible through the passenger window. If it was before noon, that would mean the window faced east and they were going north. Jake paused to reformulate the map inside his head when he saw the man pull a pistol from his jacket.

There was a bump from the rear and the car lurched forward. Jake reached to grab the gun from the man, but was held in place by his seat belt. The man turned, and noticing his efforts, swung the gun forcefully against the side of Jake's head. As Jake slumped slowly forward, he tried to form a vision of the highways going north from Paris. His thoughts, however, slowed and images mixed together as he slumped forward.

"Bordel de merde!" the driver yelled, as the man next to Jake reached over and pushed Jake's head forward, slowly to loosen the shoulder harness. He heard a screech and a loud bang, as if a small pipe bomb had exploded. Unable to make sense of what was happening, Jake reflexively pulled his arms to wrap around his head, one arm in front and the other behind his neck. He was pushed to the center of the car as it lurched sideways. There followed a slow lifting that pulled at Jake's stomach and the car rolled to the left. He flopped within the confines of his seatbelt, to the side, upside down, to the other side, right side up and then to the side and upside down once more. The car finally came to a stop, its wheels spinning in the air, with Jake hanging from his seatbelt, trying to focus on the roof now under him. He clicked on the seatbelt, and fell to the roof inside the car. He grunted as he tried to right himself in the space, the driver's headrest pressing on his shoulder. He heard a groan from the driver. As he tried to clear his vision, he saw the man next to him, unconscious but moving slowly. With the rush of adrenaline, Jake felt unscathed. In fact, he felt physically stronger and completely free of pain. Still unable to see clearly, he tried to shake his head, but was stopped when the base of his neck suddenly felt like it had been jammed by the strait-edge end of a crowbar, the pain overpowering his momentary endorphin rush. His ears began to ring loudly - low siren blasts that crescendoed to a screaming wail - yet he could hear something cracking next to him. Then a loud metallic crunch and the door beside him was yanked open a few inches. Another crunch and he saw the opposite rear seat door open. A hand reached in and snapped a handcuff to his captor, who moved feebly and ineffectively to resist. As Jake struggled to move, a metal bar crashed through the driver's side window. The driver moved around on the ceiling beneath him, still strapped with his seatbelt, now upside down. He pushed back on the deflated airbag, sweeping to find something, when Jake heard the rhythmic clicking of a taser and saw the driver's hand go slack. A second pull on the door beside him and he gained a two-foot entrance to the world. Immediately he smelled steam and radiator fluid, though his visual field was still a narrow blur.. Twisting to find his footing and crawl from the space, two hands reached in for him and pulled.

"Come, my friend. We have to hurry."

Chapter 19

Detective Martik pulled his car to the curb in front of a red three-story home in the divided block of Park Avenue in the Mount Royal neighborhood, admiring both the pristine landscaping in front of the homes and the narrow parkland which divided the north and south-bound halves of the street. Park Avenue was one of the dwindling reminders of "Old Baltimore," and Martik both understood and appreciated the tenor of the neighborhood. He reached into the passenger seat and unfolded his gray sport coat, pulled it on, and checked the breast pocket for his small notebook – a throwback to earlier times, but useful nonetheless. He glanced up and down the street, which was quiet for a mid-afternoon in Baltimore. However, schools were still in session, and he noted that Park Avenue seemed habited mostly by older couples.

Five marble steps brought him to the double front door, forest green like the window trim. The place, as would be expected in this neighborhood, was immaculate and tasteful. Without needing to knock, Martik was greeted by an older woman, thin in an athletic way and attractive in an elegant way. Her hair was dark gray and long, tied behind her head with the exception of a strand on one side which had come loose. She wore black jeans and a grey blouse, tied at the waste. She paused after opening the door to wipe some dried clay from her right hand, after which she removed a pair of half-glasses with a thin black metal frame. He reached into his breast pocket for his identification. "Melanie Daniels?"

"It's Mele, Detective Martik," she said, and when he nodded, added, "please come in, and thank you for arranging a time convenient to my teaching schedule." She moved fluidly back from the door and set her reading glasses on a small square table next to a thin coat rack.

"Of course, Mrs. Daniels, and thank you for your time." He stepped into the front room, immediately noticing the several large sculptures – both classical and abstract – which perched in the corners of the room. He moved to a sitting area, and as she motioned to a deep blue wingback chair, took a seat.

"An interesting collection of statues."

"I'm a sculptor, detective," Mrs. Daniels said, her head tilted to the side. "But I don't expect my work is involved in – well – whatever is going on."

"Yes, of course. Let me get to the point."

"Please do."

"Were you aware of the contact I had with your son Jacob on Sunday?"

"Yes, he told me about that. And I should tell you he intensely dislikes the name Jacob. Goes by Jake."

"What exactly did he tell you about our encounter?"

Mele Daniels shifted in her seat on the sofa. "I have some coffee in the kitchen. Would you like a mug?"

Martik nodded, and she left the room returning almost immediately with two mugs of coffee. "If you are wondering whether Jake told me about Luc," she said as she handed a cup to Martik and sat again on the sofa, "– yes, he did. I am horrified and saddened by tragedy, but I am not a stranger to it. Jake may have spared me some of the details, but he gave me the gist."

"I see," Martik said, taking a sip of coffee and removing his pocket notepad. "Then I'll get right to the point. I have a few additional questions for Jake, and I find that he has left the country with Ms. O'Connor. Perhaps you could tell me—"

Mele set her cup on the low table in front of the sofa. "Lily is with him? I'm sorry, detective, I guess he doesn't tell me everything after all."

"Do you happen to know their plans?"

Mele looked past Martik. "I think I know his plans, although I'm not as positive as I would have been ten seconds ago. He was – or they were. it seems – heading to Paris. He had to see someone who might be able to help explain what happened to poor Luc."

Not looking up from his notepad, Martik replied. "You are aware, I believe, Mrs. Daniels, that we have a brief record in our files on your son - specifically related to drug abuse."

Mele stiffened. "Yes, of course. And I equally believe you, Detective, are aware that his record has been spotless for the last four years."

Martik set his notepad on his lap and looked up. "Yes, I know. And I'm not looking to open any wounds with that comment. It is simply that I have a body in the morgue and two material witnesses who both seem to have left the country. I don't mean to be indelicate, but is there any chance any of this could be connected to your son's former narcotics difficulties? Anything that might give me a path to explore..."

Mele exhaled. "I understand your position, but it is a wound nonetheless. No, I can't see any possible connection to that horrible time."

"Could you add some context for me?"

"Of course." Mele leaned forward and picked up her coffee mug. took a slow sip and held the mug while resting it on her thigh. "Jake returned from Paris with a horribly damaged right hand. Several operations and two years of physical therapy followed. However, he became dependent on the pain medications, and found himself out of control. He was apprehended illegally purchasing opioids, was briefly on probation, received therapy for his addiction, and has been completely clean ever since."

"I appreciate you sharing that, Mrs. Daniels. How did he injure his hand in Paris? Was there an accident of some sort?"

Mele remained silent for a moment. "Detective, I don't think I want to talk about that."

Martik looked up from his notebook, and they both sat silently. Finally, he added, "I should tell you that I have information that is being faxed to me from the police in Paris." He let the statement hang in the air.

Mele looked down, then spoke slowly. "Jake and Luc were involved with some bad people in Paris. Quite by accident. They were competing with each other to see who could reproduce the most exact copy of an impressionist painting - I've forgotten which one. The competition was meant to be harmless. Then Luc made the foolish error of hanging their copies in the gallery he managed, and one of them was purchased by someone who thought it was an original." She paused, looking at the ceiling and breathing to control her emotions.

"And his hand?"

"Detective, the man who purchased the painting was not a good person." She paused to regain her control. "They broke into Luc's and Jake's apartment and smashed his hand so he could never paint again." She breathed once deeply. "It was terrible."

"And what happed to Luc?"

"That's all I know about Luc, detective. Jake's copy was immediately discovered still in the gallery and he was banned from submitting his work in any professional setting – even though that was unlikely to ever happen again with the injury to his hand." Mele paused, shook her head slowly, and looked up. "Seriously. That's everything." She sniffed loudly and lifted and straightened her head.

Martik closed his notebook and slipped his pen into his pocket. "I appreciate your telling me this, Mrs. Daniels. I can't imagine how difficult it must be for you to share. I will, I expect, find out about the incident from the information coming to my office, but it is incredibly helpful to hear the context from you. Incredibly helpful. And--" he stood and set his coffee mug on the low table, "I have taken enough of your time for now. I will keep you informed if I find anything new, and--" he pulled a card from his pocket, "I hope you will do the same."

Mele took the card, her hand tight to cover the hint of trembling. "Yes, of course."

Back at his office, Martik was surprised to see a folder on his desk, labeled as material faxed to him from Commissariat Central du Police du 7 Arrondisement. "That was fast," he mumbled to the empty office, leafing through the papers inside, which, he was happy to notice, were sent in English translation. He stopped on the fourth page in the folder and frowned.

He tossed the file back on his desk. "Are you shitting me?"

He walked from his office, slammed the door, and headed for the morgue.

Chapter 20

Still stumbling and his vision still clouded, Jake was maneuvered to the passenger seat of a silver Renault. Flopping uncomfortably into position, he saw an arm reach across and pull his seatbelt to fasten him in. The arm then reached down and pulled one of his feet from the pavement into the car, shutting the door. "You have to be buckled in." He turned to see a portion of a face smiling at him. "There are reckless drivers everywhere."

Jake moved to face forward and closed his eyes. "You son of a bitch," he mumbled. "I never believed it was you in the morgue -- no tattoo." His eyes still closed, he ran his tongue over his lips. "Got any water?"

Luc handed him a small plastic bottle, and Jake sipped slowly. "We have a lot to talk about."

"No shit," Jake mumbled, and, squinting, opened his eyes. "Let's start with 'where are we going' and 'how are we going to get Lily'." Jake turned slightly to the driver's side. "Then you can get to the minor stuff, like 'what the hell is going on'."

"We are driving to Romigny. I have a work studio there, and I think that is where we can find Lily." Luc shook his head. "This should not have gone so far. I'm incredibly sorry to have pulled both of you into this mess - it was not my intention."

"Bit late for apologies."

"Yes, I know. My plan was to leave the painting with you and contact the authorities in DC. Then I'm ambushed by this man and he's taking me by gunpoint to who-knows-where. So there is an opportunity - a minor distraction - and I duck under him. We wrestle a bit and the gun goes off. And, well, he's dead."

Jake paused, the bottle nearly to his lips. "Nobody around?"

Luc shrugged. "He is taking me to a place very deserted. I simply made use of his own precautions."

Jake nodded. "I get it." He shifted in his seat, his vision clearing a bit more. "So you stripped and switched clothes? That sounds awkward."

"I had rented a car. Stored him in the trunk and drove off to one of the abandoned harbor warehouses. Not really a problem."

Jake fought back his roiling anger. "And the face?"

Luc shrugged. "Some muriatic acid from Home Depot. Not meant to be a permanent fake - just enough to buy some time." And I altered his hair color and did some cutting." After a pause, he added, "And thank you for not informing the police. I am curious, however. Why did the police come to you? Did Lily inform them?"

Jake looked to his left. "Stop pretending. My address was tucked into your goddamn shoe."

Luc frowned as he drove. "Putain," he mumbled. "That was careless of me."

"King of the understatement." Jake flexed and rolled his shoulders, reaching back to rub his neck. "So do you have some sort of plan at Romigny? Even a

129

careless one?" He straitened in his seat, stretched his head forward and took another sip of water. "How do you know she's there and how hard will it be to get her out? And do you have any aspirin here?"

Luc nodded to the glove compartment. "A bottle in there. They are not extra strength, so take two."

"I'll take four if it's all the same to you." Jake shook aspirin out of the bottle and swallowed them with another drink of water. He felt in his pocket, noticing that his own pill bottle was still there. He caressed the cylindrical shape and the quick snap cap. They were easy to remove and take, but he thought better of it. "Who is holding her, and what have you gotten into? Someone tried to kill you, others followed us in Paris, someone captured Lily at the apartment and still others were hustling me off somewhere. How far does this go?

"That is a lot of questions."

"Oh that's just the beginning. But I'll start with an easy one. Who are you working with and who was that guy who cuffed and stayed behind at the crash?"

As Luc stared silently at the road ahead, Jake waited. The pause became a hold and became a silence. Jake had cleared his head enough to feel the tug on that door he had held closed in his head since Luc's first appearance at his houseboat. Or had it been shut for years, he wondered. "Luc... cut the shit," he responded with a growled command.

Luc shook his head and sighed heavily. "My friend, I'm sorry to tell you this." He swallowed. "His name is Jean Nichol. He's with the FBI International

Operations Division- the IOD. You know how government agencies like initials. He is working with the French Legat – the Legal Attache', and is a good friend, and can be trusted, I promise you." With that, Luc reset his attention on the road ahead.

"And?" Jake said. "What else? You just said a lot about this guy without really telling me anything. And you certainly aren't sorry to tell me he's with the FBI. I figured that already. So who is he?" his voice rising.

"Jean," Luc began and paused again, "is Lily's husband."

The door in Jake's mind flew open so quickly he was unprepared for the white-hot fury within. Physically struggling, his eyes shut tight, he pushed the door closed once again. "Of course," he heard himself mumble, wondering if Luc had heard him too. It had been five years. Lily was a captivating, intelligent, beautiful woman. To think her life would be unchanged, to think she would be waiting for her lost Paris lover to somehow return someday, or even just to contact her, was naivety in the extreme. "Okay," he said, exhaling. "At least I know."

Luc turned to look at him. "There is more you don't know, but that is not for now. We have more pressing matters. And I've convinced Jean that I'm taking you to a safe location – that should provide us some opportunity to do this properly."

"Properly?"

"Yes, with the least risk for Lily. I know what has to be done, and I'm not sure the FBI does."

"Shit," Jake said, laying a heavy blanket of sadness over the word. "Okay. This guy you pissed off. He tried to have you killed. He had Lily and me followed on the plane to Paris. We were tagged again on the streets. They broke into your apartment and then ambushed us there. There was a fight and I killed somebody, and even when I got lucky and managed to almost escape, two others arrived to haul me away. That's two dead, two now captured by the FBI from the car crash, and," he paused, "Again, I'm asking, how many others? Who is in charge and what kind of manpower does he - or she - have ready to go after all of us?" Jake paused, and then added, "And I assume this is all about that damned Pissarro?"

"The Pissarro is only the tip of the iceberg. You really killed one of them? I'm sorry for that, also. But please know that whichever one he was he would certainly have killed you if you didn't prevail. Don't feel guilty about that."

"I don't," Jake said, a bit surprised how clearly he meant it.

After another minute of silence as Jake closed his eyes and rubbed the back of his neck, Luc said, "The man in charge of all of this calls himself the Collector, and there are many more who work for him, I'm afraid."

"The Collector? Are you serious? That's a comic book name."

"Does sound that way, but he guards his identity very carefully."

Jake looked over at Luc and waited. "So who is he?"

"His name is Wilson. Peter Wilson. And he is very rich and very powerful and very, very aggressive - perhaps psychopathic."

Luc paused. Jake said, "Don't stop now."

"He collects art - and has quite an extensive collection."

"So does my mother."

"No. Not like this. His collection is centered on those pieces he has looted and stolen - sometimes from individuals or galleries and sometimes from museums."

Jake looked ahead at the road, piecing information together. "Including pieces you forged for him and then switched with the originals?"

Luc nodded. "Yes, I did that twice for him."

"Shit, Luc!" Silence followed as Jake considered. After a minute of quiet driving, he said. "So are we going to this studio in Romigny because you think Lily is there?"

"Yes, I do. I think Lily is--" Luc paused. "-- the word. Bait. Yes, I think Lily is bait."

Jake shook his head. "Jesus. Who's the catch? You? Me? The Pissarro?"

"All of these, I'm quite sure, although there is a chance he doesn't know yet that I'm still alive. That may be helpful."

They covered another kilometer silently before Jake said, his eyes closed again, "So are we going empty-handed?"

Luc smiled. "There is a metal box on the floor behind your seat."

Chapter 21

For the second time that day, Detective Martik pulled his car to the cub at Park Avenue, removed his jacket from the back seat and put it on, checked his notebook, and looked up the steps to the front door of the Daniels' home. This time the door was answered by a tall man with dark curly hair, dusted with the first bits of gray. Reading glasses hung from a string around his neck.

As the door opened, Martik removed his ID wallet. "Harrison Daniels? I'm Detective Martik with the Southeast District, Baltimore Police. I spoke earlier today with your wife, but we haven't met."

"Yes, Mele told me all about it," the man said in a quiet bass voice, stepping to the side of the open door as a gesture for Martik to enter. "You have more questions?"

"A few, yes. But I do want to share some new information, Mr. Daniels."

"Call me Harris, please, detective. Mele has finished her classes for the day and I've just arrived from the Walters, so you have us both. That's sometimes difficult to do."

Martik walked into the living room and, noting a gesture from Harris, assumed his place in the same wingback chair he had occupied earlier. "Yes, fortunate timing, I suppose. You are head curator of sculpture at the Walters Art Gallery, right? That must be a very time-consuming position."

"Well, not nearly as time-consuming as homicide detective in downtown Baltimore, I imagine," Harris said as he sat on the sofa.

Mele arrived from the kitchen and stopped suddenly when she saw Martik. Harris rose from the sofa for his wife, but she spoke first. "Detective, can I assume you came back for a coffee refill?"

Martik smiled. "It was good."

"Then I'll be right back," she said as she exited for the kitchen.

Harris studied Martik. "Let's wait until she returns. It won't be but a minute and I want her to be in on whatever information you have for us." Then he leaned forward. "But tell me. Is Jake okay?"

"I don't have any information about that, Mr. Daniels."

Mele returned with two coffee mugs, gave one to Martik and one to Harris, and sat cross-legged on the sofa next to her husband. "What is it detective?"

"Well, when I returned to my office, there was an envelope of information that had been faxed from Paris."

"He's trying to find out who might have killed Luc," Mele said to her husband.

"Hold that thought, Mrs. Daniels. It could very well be that no one killed Lucas Benoit."

Mele and Harris straightened in unison. "But didn't Jake identify the body in the morgue?" Harris added.

Martik took a long sip of coffee, deliberately letting the confusion linger as he watched the couple's reaction. "The body in the morgue is not Lucas Benoit.

Information from Paris confirms that. I don't know who it is in my morgue, but I know who it isn't – and it isn't Lucas Benoit."

There was another silence as the couple looked at each other. "But how could Jake have been so confused? And you said Lily was there also," Mele said.

"Yes. They both ID'd him. And now they're both gone." Martik was slowing the conversation deliberately as he studied the reactions and body language of the couple. "One other thing," he said, continuing to speak slowly. "The Paris report included identifying marks – it's standard procedure – and the only thing provided was a tattoo on the left side of the chest, just below the collarbone. Of course, there is no such tattoo on our body in the morgue." He paused again. "I'm telling you this because, before he identified the body as Luc, your son asked me to move the covering sheet to expose the top of the torso." Martik sat back in the chair and sipped again at his coffee, watching the couple closely.

The silence continued for nearly a full minute. Harris Daniels broke it with, "Detective Martik. I – I just don't know what to say."

Mele looked at Martik and then at her husband. "So... he knew?" she said to her husband, her voice dry..

Martik set his coffee mug on the small table and sat back. "Look, Mr. and Mrs. Daniels – I believe that you have no idea what is going on. I wasn't sure of that an hour ago, but I am now."

"Thank you," Mele said in a whisper, holding Harris' hand tightly in hers.

"I've been on the force long enough to hone a few instincts about people, Mrs. Daniels. and my instinct is telling me you are both as surprised by this as I am, and," he shifted in his seat, "that brings me to the second reason for coming."

Harris leaned forward. "There's more?"

"Much more, in fact. The fact that it isn't Lucas Benoit in the morgue means that someone either tried to kill him and failed or tried to make it look as though he had – or 'she' I suppose. And for some reason, your son was drawn into this. As was the FBI agent Lily O'Connell – who I find gave me a false name and is listed with the FBI under her married name - Lily Nicol."

"Lily?" Harris said. "Married?"

"And so they both suddenly leave for Paris – flying first class on the Bureau's dime – knowing they were leaving as witnesses to an active homicide investigation. Does that strike you as normal behavior for an FBI agent?"

Harris and Mele both shook their heads.

"Now that same instinct is telling me that you two might be in some danger here. Clearly, there are people involved – both in Europe and here in Baltimore. That indicates some level of organization rather than an individual working on his or her own.. It seems clear that they have some power, and just as clear that your son was anxious to get as far away from you both as he could – and as soon as he could." Martik paused to let things sink in.

Harris looked over at Mele and pulled her hand into his lap. "What can we do to help?"

Martik held his pencil to his notebook. "Let's start with Sunday. Jake left my office shortly after one o'clock. Did he come by here at all?"

Mele responded immediately. "Yes, but not until the evening, perhaps about 8 or 8:30. I remember because we were having a glass of wine and we asked if he wanted to join us. He said he couldn't but that he had to go to Paris and check into Luc's belongings."

Harris added. "He called in the afternoon, and we talked for about a half hour. When he came by in the evening, he just had an overnight carry-on and his passport. Said he'd be back in a day or two." Harris looked at the floor. "We had no idea."

"Just a carry-on and passport? Did he leave anything with you?"

"No," Harris said, but then Mele poked him.

"Actually yes, detective."

Martik perked up. "What? What was it?"

Mele turned her head to the kitchen and whistled airily. Bromo walked into the room, shaking his head as if just waking up. "This is Bromo. Jake's dog. He left him here with us."

Bromo walked over to Martik, sniffed, and sat, his tail wagging. "We've already met," he said, reaching down to rub behind Bromo's ears. The dog's eyes closed to contented slits. "But was there anything else?"

Mele and Harris looked at each other. "Nothing," Harris said. "Sorry, but nothing."

Martik closed his notebook and stood. "Mrs. Daniels, do you still have my card?"

"Of course."

"I want you both to put that phone number into your contact lists. And if you see anyone lurking outside or looking at your home, call me immediately. That's my cell phone and I can be here in under three minutes. I will also have someone watching the street as often as possible - sometimes marked and sometimes unmarked. I don't want to alarm your neighbors. But that doesn't mean you two. In your case, a bit of alarm will keep you alert. If you even have a gut feeling that you should call, do it. If I'm on the other side of town someplace, I'll have a colleague here even faster." Martik paused to make sure they were following him. "And if it is awkward to call me, just hit the contact button. You don't have to say anything - or even hold the phone up. I'll be on my way."

"Should we be scared?" Mele said, "because we can take pretty good care of ourselves. This might be going overboard. It sounds like a lot of false alarms to me."

Martik looked directly at her. "No, I don't want you to be scared. But I do want you to be careful. Also, I'll have someone keep a close watch at the Walters and at MICA, if you will please give me your work schedules. I'll make sure to keep things discreet. But the point is we don't know what's happening yet. And whoever that is in my morgue could probably take care of himself, too. And lastly, I don't mind false alarms at all. Not one bit. What I hate is the real alarm that doesn't get said." He paused. "Are you with me on this? I need you to be with me. 100 percent."

Mele and Harris looked at each other for a moment. "Of course, detective," Harris said as Martik nodded and turned to leave.

"And, of course, call me if anything occurs to you that we haven't discussed, or if Jake contacts you."

Chapter 22

Moving off the highway onto local roads as they approached Romigny, the air seemed to shift, as if the highway had taken them to an earlier and milder time. Jake squinted and covered his eyes in the sunlight as they drove past scattered stone buildings with red roofs, nested close to the road and fronting rows of vines that stretched over the soft rolls of the countryside, ending at some distant perspective point. The yellow mustard flowers were in full bloom between many of the rows, for those growers who had adopted the practice as a means of gauging the proper time to manage the fruit sets that had recently appeared in clusters, pulling the vines earthward. He noticed vineyard crews working the rows, arranging the clusters and the vines draping over them.

"Are they arranging the grape canopies already? Isn't it early for that?"

Although historically at the center of the Champagne region in France, recent small shifts in the local climate had opened the door for many possibilities, as vineyards looked to protect their investment with those diverse grape varieties showing promise as blending grapes in warmer climates.

"Looks like they are. Global warming, I suppose." Luc pulled the car into a cut-out along the side of the road. "Let's plan this - specifically, I mean."

Jake reached behind and pulled out the metal box. Inside he saw three handguns and several boxes of ammunition. "Dammit, guns aren't going to help. They're going to get one of us killed - or all of us." Jake looked into the box in the silence that followed. "Dammit, Luc, what is this? Yes, I know which end of a gun is the business end, but I'm not any sort of weapons expert, and I have no intention of pretending to be one."

Luc turned and pointed to the items in the box. "The two are Sig Sauers. Very highly regarded by your military, by the way. Both have gun grips so they won't slip in your hand – even if you are, well, sweating a bit. Each has a clip loaded with eleven rounds, with three spare clips."

"You learned all this from your work in an art gallery? What aren't you telling me?" Luc said nothing as he pulled back onto the road, and after a long pause, Jake pointed to the third gun. "And this one?"

"The revolver is a snub-nose 38. Not as effective."

"And why do you have three?"

"Plans change." Luc looked directly at Jake. "The Sig should conceal nicely in the waist of your pants, with a clip in your pocket. Do you know about safeties?"

Jake nodded. "A gun in my pants pocket? Is this some sort of game for you?"

Luc ignored him. "So here's what we need to do. Well, you actually. I have to stay hidden, since Wilson hopefully thinks I'm dead. As I said, that can be an advantage. The building is small, has no windows in the main section, and one window in the door of the back room where I believe we will find Lily."

"Okay, but that is just a lay-out, it isn't a plan. Who is going to be there waiting for us – or for me?"

"Wilson will be there, probably, unless he wants to deal with you remotely via camera. A guard for Lily and perhaps two more."

"Camera? How many cameras and where are you going to be? And what should I expect from the guy – Wilson? He wants to trade Lily for the painting?"

Luc thought for a moment, then shook his head. "No, I think he wants more. The painting, of course, but I had started a project for him – an Alfred Sisley – and I think he would like you to finish it. And just one camera – inside the structure."

Jake looked over at Luc. "You're kidding, right? He wants me to finish copying some work by Sisley so that he can make a switch and add the real painting to his collection? Come on, Luc, I'm sure this guy has access to any number of talented art copiers who can forge a Sisley. What makes him think for a minute that I would do it? Or even that I could do it? Aren't these the guys who smashed my hand five years ago!"

Luc gave a light shrug. "I'm sure he knows you have recovered and are still competent. As I mentioned to you back on your boat, you are easily Googled, and The Coll—Wilson is a meticulous man. And why would you do it? He has Lily – that's all."

Jake turned to face the front, and thought for a moment. "No, he doesn't want me to paint anything. There another angle working here. And if he knows all about me, he probably also knows that his two goons didn't make it here with me."

"Perhaps he knows that also, but I can assure you he doesn't care. Those who work for him are carefully chosen and well-paid, but he thinks nothing of them. You are here and that will be his focus. And is there another way? Yes, my friend! The way is this." He patted the gun now tucked into his waistband. All we have to do is get Lily free. Jean and the FBI will be here before much longer, and they can take it from there. But we have to do this first, to make sure Lily is safe."

"So I walk in there and, after a little angry acting, agree to his plan. What about you?"

"I'll be outside. There will likely be guards there to warn of your approach, since there are no windows – and that camera I mentioned is only inside the studio. I'll make sure the guards don't come inside."

"How?"

Luc shrugged. "I just will. And when that is taken care of, and you have Wilson's attention – with your angry acting - I'll come around to the rear and get Lily out of there."

Jake, still staring ahead, running the video in his mind, added, "And the guard on Lily?"

Luc shrugged. "I'll take care of that, also."

Checking the thumb safety, Jake tucked the handgun into his back pocket and shook his head. "First of all, I goddam know you aren't telling me everything – hell, you probably aren't even telling me most of it. And second, that is a shit plan."

Chapter 23

Martik parked on Bond Street two blooks from where he was to meet Agent Fallsborough. It was a quiet residential street, and he wanted to enjoy the pleasure of walking to the tavern on the corner, enjoying the early evening air off the harbor and taking a moment to collect his thoughts. He wasn't sure he was playing the correct card here, but – he shrugged – sometimes you just have to play something. The streets were quiet, as was the tavern itself, which Martik knew opened for the few daily beer and breakfast patrons. He stepped to the entrance, checking his pockets to make sure he was without any of the ornaments of his career. No gun, no badge or official ID. Not even his small notepad. Stepping in, he saw Fallsborough seated at a table in the rear, chosen at least in part because no one was seated nearby. Martik pulled out a chair and sat across from him.

"No suit and tie!" Martik tried to offer a welcoming smile. "I'm glad you came out of uniform."

"As you requested, detective. But why the incognito gambit? You don't look like a person who is comfortable 'out of uniform,' as you describe it." Fallsborough paused. "I assume we are officially off-duty."

"Absolutely. And to seal the deal, I'm having a beer – something you could certainly report me for if we weren't off-duty." He turned and signaled the bartender, pointing to one of the taps. "So are we good, then? We can talk off the record?"

Fallsborough smiled and looked over at the bar. "What do you suggest?"

"Evolution IPA – on tap. It's a local favorite for before-noon beers."

Two tall and wide glasses arrived almost immediately, sporting a perfect one-inch head and already sweating. Each took a long sip and a pause followed.

"So, detective," Fallsborough ran his finger over the rim of his glass. "You called this undercover meeting. Can you tell me why?"

Martik nodded. "Yes." He took another sip and slid his glass aside. "I've worked with the FBI before, and I know your need to keep everything in-house. I also know that, the longer this takes, the more likely it is that you will stop by with an envelope of paperwork, and I will say goodbye to you and to whomever it is lying in my morgue. Then I'll be required to file the paperwork to make the whole thing go away from this end."

Fallsborough nodded. "Tomorrow, most likely. Transport has already arrived."

Martik nodded. "But I also did a little research. I know that you were a municipal detective at one point – not so very long ago. Utica, New York, wasn't it?" Martik didn't look up to notice Fallsborough nodding. "So I know that you remember how it feels to have a case pulled out from under you by a higher jurisdiction. It feels like shit."

Fallsborough was still nodding. "Yes, it does. I've been on the receiving end more than once. Sorry, it does feel like shit – but you know that is how this is going to go."

"Yes. I will have to turn over the body and any items found on or with it." Martik looked directly at Fallsborough. "But I don't have to turn over my notes, my observations, my auxiliary findings."

Fallsborough took another long sip and waited.

"But I would like to turn over those things. I would like to see this murder solved, even if it isn't by me. So I want a trade. I want to augment your information and I want you to augment my curiosity."

"Meaning what, exactly. I can't just tell you everything. You know that."

"Yea, I know. But here's the thing: I have two witnesses in an open homicide investigation currently out of the country. I fully expect, however, that they will return. I would like to know what to do at that point. Who was – or is – Lucas Benoit? Is Jacob Daniels a player involved in something I need to be aware of? And how do I avoid entangling myself and my time with your investigation? Not only that, but Daniels' parents are local citizens and good people. Do I have to be concerned for their safety - because right now I am."

"That's a lot."

"Fair enough. Try this: Can you tell me why you were investigating Benoit? Is there something happening here in Baltimore that I need to be aware of?"

"In fact, detective, we weren't actively investigating Benoit. That investigation concluded a short time ago. However, the inquiry revealed other things."

"Then, in all due respect, agent – what the hell is going on?"

"I can tell you this: We are investigating agent Lily Nicole."

Martik paused and looked away to take in the new information.

"Yes, I can't give you much in the way of detail, but agent Nicole is into something pretty bad – or so it appears, and it revealed itself in her investigation of Benoit. She may even have something to do with the body in your morgue, detective. Jacob Daniels may well return to Baltimore, and you can question him or not as you please. But if agent Nicole is with him, I can assure you she will not leave the airport without our escort."

Martik took another sip and nodded. "Got me there," he said quietly. "Didn't see that coming." Then after a moment he looked directly at Fallsborough. "So is there a Baltimore angle to this? What should I be looking for in my city?"

Fallsborough thought for a minute. "I don't really know. Sorry, but that's the truth. I will tell you this, however: I'll be stationed here for a time in the chance of apprehending agent Nicole. If anything comes my way regarding criminal activities in the city, I'll call you. That's a promise."

Martik reached out and shook hands with the agent. "We share information, then. No need to go undercover."

"No need to go undercover - agreed," said Fallsborough. "Although I have to admit, I enjoyed the ale." He smiled as Martik set a few bills on the table and they rose to leave. "An excellent breakfast beverage."

Chapter 24

What seemed like half an hour later – although there was no clock in the car to verify his instincts – they crunched onto a gravel parking area in front of a simple cement block warehouse. The building was indeed windowless, was painted a deep gray and was so nondescript one could scan the scene and not even register its presence. Emerging from the driver's side after letting Luc out about a hundred yards back, Jake paused, removed the gun from his pocket and left it on the seat. He looked to see two men outside the door to the building – one sitting on a metal chair and the other leaning against the structure. The two looked at each other and the one leaning against the building stood upright and removed a white cell phone, making a call that seemed to last for only a few seconds. Jake walked forward slowly; his arms raised slightly so that his open palms were shoulder high.

The two pulled small guns from beneath their jackets, moving with an ease rooted in extreme confidence. The one who had been sitting punched a code and opened the door. As Jake stepped in, one man flicked a light switch, gave a quick and experienced pat-down to Jake's clothing and turned to leave, closing the door behind him. Suddenly awash in light, the inside was as nondescript as the outside had been. Bare walls, painted off-white, revealed the shadows of prior use – a rectangular mark from an earlier picture frame, the base of a water cooler, a few chairs scattered through the space. Half of the floor was carpeted in what appeared to be an indoor-outdoor material. The floor of the back half of the structure was bare concrete, clearly a work area. Several canvasses were stacked against the wall, as were several different wood panels – either very old or artificially aged to appear antique. One had been partially sanded to accept paint. A large reddish-brown stain on the carpeting near the wall on Jake's right might have been a spilled cup of coffee, or a tinting compound – or something else. Off to the left of center, a small wooden desk was decorated by a land-line style phone console.

Nothing happened.

Jake stood, looking intently at the closed door in the rear of the large space. Scanning where the walls met the ceiling, the small video camera was easy to spot. A shrill alarm broke the silence and he jumped before realizing the console phone on the desk was ringing. Trying not to let his hesitation reveal any emotion, and deliberately waiting for the third ring, Jake picked up the receiver.

"Mr. Daniels?"

"Uh-huh," Jake replied.

"Come on now, Mr. Daniels. Let's not be coy. You know why you are here and you know what I want." The voice was older, probably American but with slight overtones of someone who had spent much of his life in England. His speaking style was slow and measured, as if he considered every word before uttering it. "Or, to be more specific, what I did want. I now find that I want two things from you. First, I want the Pissarro."

Jake was expecting something more dramatic, certainly more threatening in tone, but still paused to consider his options. "The Pissarro. You mean the real one? Otherwise, you could go visit the fake at the d'Orsey any time you wanted. You can even get a membership so admission will be free. Tell you what - let's make a trade. I want—"

"I do not do 'deals,' Mr. Daniels." The voice raised in timbre, but was still very controlled, accenting each syllable. "I want my painting, and that is the end of the first part of our arrangement."

"*Your* painting?" Jake said, finding it easier than he had anticipated to maintain an air of confidence. "That's a bit absurd, isn't it?"

"Not at all. I paid for that painting. At least I paid Mr. Benoit to obtain it for me. Paid him well, I might add." There was a pause on the line.

"Without the return of Lily O'Connell you'll never see that painting again."

There was a brief silence, followed by a sigh clearly audible over the phone. "Mr. Daniels, you are mistaken. I will get my painting back. If you won't help, then I'm sure I can convince your mother or father to assist in this." There was a pause. "You do understand, don't you?" Another pause and then the voice returned. "But as I said, I now find that I want two things."

Jake's pulse had quickened with the mention of his parents, and icy fingers seemed to paw at his back; but knowing there was a camera he held himself in check and shook his head. "What else then?" Jake said, trying not to sound defeated – and purposefully failing.

"Mr. Benoit spoke fondly of you before, sadly, he passed. However, I have also done some research and I find it serendipitous that you are perhaps the perfect man to finish a project for me."

"Work for you? You are kidding, right?" Jake tried not to yell into the phone and found his response hoarse.

"Yes, but not without compensation. Upon satisfactory completion of this work – and the return of my painting – I will let you go your way and I will return Ms. O'Connell to you. Not a bad arrangement, you must agree."

"You don't expect me to believe that you'll set us both free if I do this for you. It's too late for that, don't you think?"

"Not at all." The man paused and spoke more slowly. "You don't know me – you have only met a few of my employees. You even managed to kill one of them, so I think I'm being very forgiving on that matter. Ms. O'Connell knows even less than you. My project is rather specific and requires your particular set of talents. Your training and expertise should allow you to finish your work in a short time – perhaps a matter of a few days."

"Go to hell. There is no way I'm doing anything for you."

The reply was louder and angrier. "Listen closely, Daniels. You have no cards to play here. You and

O'Connell are either dead or not. And with a snap of my fingers your mother's and father's deaths will be on your conscience." He paused and again lowered his voice to a conversational tone. "So grow up and think this through. All things considered, it's a good arrangement for you."

Jake held his anger in check as he thought of all the pain this man could cause with apparent ease. At the rear of the room, the door opened slightly. Peripherally, out of respect for the camera trained on him, Jake could see Luc's face look out from the door, and a gesture for him to follow. "Yes, it is a good arrangement." He exhaled and shook his head, as if shaking off the last of his self-respect. "What do you need?"

And in the pause that followed the question, Jake ran for the rear exit, jumping over the still form of a large man face down on the floor and around the building to the car – where Luc was in the rear seat with the driver's door opened for Jake. Lily was in the passenger seat, slumped over. "Some sort of sedative, I think," Luc said. "She seems unharmed but we have to get out of here."

As they were turning to pull away from the parking area, a sedan pulled into the entrance and the two guards from before jumped out, guns in hand.

Luc leaned forward. "Jake, listen carefully. I can get their attention – I will be your distraction, so that you and Lily escape. I'll find you later at Ghent. Do you know how to get there? Ghent. Belgium. Get to the center of old city and I'll contact you. Trust me on this. Go now." With that he jumped from the car. Yelling something at the two men, Luc pointed to the building, gesticulating wildly. The two guards quickly turned and ran to the building as Jake hit the gas, pulled around the sedan, and off onto the streets of Romigny.

As they sped away, Jake reached into his pocket, removed his personal phone, still turned off from their arrival in Paris, and rummaged deeper into his pocket, behind the pill bottle, for Martik's business card. He looked over at Lily, who seemed to be sleeping quietly. "Dammit, Luc," he whispered. One hand on the wheel, he punched in the numbers.

Chapter 25

It was nearly two hours later, just outside of Lille and nearing the border with Belgium that Lily stirred and began to wake. Jake pulled over into one of the truck stops along the A1, and held Lily's hand as she opened her eyes – lost and then puzzled and then wide.

"Hey," Jake said, glancing to Lily and then releasing her hand and looking ahead as he drove back on to the highway. "You there, now?"

Lily squirmed to sit up straight, held her hands to her eyes, and then squinted as she looked ahead. "Um-hm. What's happened? Where are we going?"

Jake took a deep breath. "Lots to tell you. We're heading for Ghent. You were sedated." Without looking over, he handed a plastic bottle of water to her.

"Thanks," she mumbled, talking a long drink, some of the water dripping onto her chin. "I remember hitting somebody with something. Pretty hard. Then the injection. Then nothing." Lily looked out the window at the passing countryside, small houses dotting the view with quickening frequency as they left the highway and neared the border town of Dronkaard. "What can you tell me?"

"A lot, but not yet. I want to make sure you're with it. Sit tight for a bit."

Lily looked over, noticing that Jake did not return her glance. Pursing her lips, she looked ahead. She closed her eyes to rub behind her head, but felt dizziness almost immediately and forced her eyes open. Jake continued to drive, not speaking.

The next hour was lost in silence.

As they drove into the Ghent town center, Lily looked to see the old city, it's winding streets lined with three-story shops and apartments. Off-white stone and stucco façades, each decorated with an elaborate array of low-relief sculptures and pilasters. The step-gabled rooflines added the Dutch ambience that she would have loved to savor – at another time. She turned to Jake. "Okay, so we're here. Time to talk?" Her silence had grown into exasperation and annoyance, and her tone did little to hide either.

"Yeah, OK. I just want to find a coffee shop. We haven't had anything since this morning. You need some food and some caffeine – and so do I. We could also use an internet connection." Still focusing his attention entirely on the road, Jake pulled into a side street just off the Botemarkt in Ghent Center. Leaving the car, they walked silently to a café at the corner.

"Ah, here." Jake said, walking inside and sitting at one of the small tables with a public computer tablet on a small stand. A young woman came to the table, and both Jake and Lily ordered sandwiches and coffee.

"Enough already," Lily began. "What's happening? Are we still working together on something or have I been kidnapped for a second time in one day?"

Jake looked up at her. "You could have told me."

"There is a lot I didn't tell you," she said without the slightest hint of apology. "What in particular could I have told you?" The question was a challenge.

"That you were married, for one."

"Oh," Lily looked at the table top. "That."

"Not that I had any right to know."

"True. You didn't."

"But we could have discussed it."

"I didn't want to." She looked directly at Jake. "I still don't."

In the silence that followed, Jake opened the computer to a server screen, his anger leaking in a slow hiss. "Sorry," he said, looking away from the computer and back to Lily. "You're right. I have no business in your private life." He exhaled. "I gave up that right long ago. I know."

"Some day, Jake," she said. "But not today. Fill me in on what's happening."

Jake gave a detailed overview of the time since his return from the Musee d'Orsay, including the crash and re-appearance of Luc - their drive to Romigny, and the sketchy plan that didn't turn out to be much of a plan at all. "Your husband – Jean – was with Luc and was part of the car crash. He stayed behind with the two gunmen. I'm guessing he and others from the FBI have arrived at the studio by now."

Lily replied with a brief account of her own. She was surprised and overpowered when two men were waiting for her in Luc's apartment. She confirmed using the name 'Jacob' to warn him, and was drugged immediately after the phone call. She regained consciousness briefly at the studio in Romigny, where she was being watched by the same man who had forced her to answer Jake's call at the apartment. She then described a disturbance in the room outside of where she was being held, and took advantage of the distraction to smash a full can of some chemical into the man's head, who then toppled forward, only bending slightly at one knee, causing him to fall on his side. He hit the floor loud and hard, bouncing slightly. Someone came behind her and then all went black again. There was a pause as each took in the other's encounter. "Some guy, Peter Wilson, who calls himself 'The Collector'? Really? And Luc not only re-appears from the dead, but saves the day and tells you that he will meet us here? Are you serious? Why here?"

"We're in Ghent. We're dealing with theft and forgery." Jake paused as sandwiches and coffee arrived, taking a sip before jolting. "Careful. It's hot. Access your art history. There can only be one reason he told me to come to Ghent."

Lily's eyes widened and her mouth framed an "O." "Of course. The Mystic Lamb. The Ghent altarpiece."

"Tell me what you know, historically," Jake said as he set the translation function on the computer screen to English. "But fast forward to World War I."

Lily took a bite from her sandwich and followed with a sip of coffee. "Okay -- The altarpiece, created in the early 1400s by Hubert and Jan van Eyck – although Jan van Eyck gets the credit for most of the work – is right up there with the Mona Lisa and the Sistine Chapel as a wonder of the art world. I hate to admit I've never come here to see it, despite living only a few hours away for all this time. Anyway, it has eight exterior panels, and when you unfold it, it has twelve interior panels.

"Have to confess, I haven't seen it in person, either," Jake said, still typing. "although I'm guessing that's about to change."

Lily looked up and continued. "The panels of the altarpiece have been separated, and looted and stolen on several occasions, going all the way back to the Reformation. But here's the fast-forward. Prior to World War I - back in the 1800s - some panels were sold to some collector in Germany, and then bought again by the German king - what's-his-name."

Jake looked up.

"Hey, if you want names, go to Wikipedia." Lily took another bite. "During the war, additional panels found their way to Germany - legitimately or otherwise - depends on who you ask. Then these were all sent back to Belgium in 1918, as part of Germany's reparations after the Armistice. A lot of German resentment about that. Next, as things were heating up prior to World War II, two of the panels went missing, although when, exactly isn't clear. The remaining panels were moved and hidden to try and keep them out of Nazi hands, but that effort failed. Hitler's war machine found them and demanded they be brought to Bavaria. Because of allied air raids, however, Hitler had them stored – first in Mad Ludwig's castle in Bavaria – Neuschwanstein – and then in a salt mine, which is where allied troops found them. It was a major part of the story of the Monuments Men."

Jake was tapping away. "What do you know about the two stolen panels during the war?"

"Not much. One was found and returned shortly after the war ended, the panel depicting John the Baptist. The other, and I can't remember the topic of it, was never found and was replaced with a copy." Lily suddenly sat up straight and looked at Jake. "The copy was made by van Vesten, or something like that. He was an expert forger who had been implicated also in art theft - although never proven. Is that a connection?" She leaned across the small table to look at the computer screen. Jake pulled his chair over and she moved in next to him.

"Here it is," Jake said. Jeff Van der Veken. Apparently, he was an expert forger of the early Netherlandish and Dutch painters. Some of his forgeries even passed as originals. He started the copy of that missing panel – referred to as The Just Judges – in 1934, and then finished it at the war's end."

"But what's the connection?"

"The connection is this, he must have done this forgery on commission. Nobody goes to that much trouble purely out of the goodness of his heart – especially not a guy like Van der Veken. And --" he paused, hitting a few key strokes, "-- look who paid him! Follow the money, right?"

Lily leaned closer to read the text at the bottom of the screen. "Oh my God," she whispered, suddenly alert to anyone nearby. "Alexander Wilson. Seriously?" Looking at Jake, she added, "but Wilson is a pretty common name, right? Could be a coincidence."

Jake clicked and pointed. "True, but here's the obituary for Alexander Wilson - big time financier. Desk job during the war – made Lieutenant Colonel, apparently. Then helped with several art restorations in Europe after the war. And take a guess at his one surviving offspring."

"Peter," Lily said exhaling as she read. "Peter Wilson."

A ring tone came from the pocket of the fleece jacket Jake had rolled up under his sleeve. "What the hell?" he said, startled, as he fumbled into the fleece ball. On the third ring, he pulled an old flip-top style phone from the pocket. Looking at Lily, and receiving nothing but a concerned shrug in return, he flipped the top. "Yea?"

"Jake, are you in Ghent? Are you both safe?"

"Yes, Luc, what now?" Jake held the phone so that Lily could lean in and hear. "Where are you?"

"Can't explain much right now. I slipped the phone into your pocket while hustling you into the car after Romigny. I'll arrive in Ghent sometime overnight. And tell Lily, Jean is with me. We are playing quiet to catch some bigger fish – I think that is the phrase. So get some rest for a busy day tomorrow. We'll meet you both at the coffee shop under the white awning on the square in front of St Bavo's. Eight tomorrow morning. The cathedral opens at 8:30. All good?"

Jake pursed his lips and paused. "Yea, all good."

"Good. Bonne nuit."

Lily squinted as she looked at Jake. "I want this over."

Jake looked at Lily, nodded, leaned back and reached for his sandwich. After a pause, he looked back at the computer screen. "Peter fucking Wilson."

Chapter 26

"Mr. Daniels. This is Detective Martik. I would like to speak with you and Mrs. Daniels. At your son's houseboat. Perhaps in an hour?"

"Detective – do you have--" Harris fought his anxiety and mimicked Martik's flattened speaking style. "-- any information about our son?" Harris fought to hide both the anxiety and excitement from his voice, mimicking the flat tones of Martik's greeting without realizing it. "What's happened?"

"Yes, I do have some information for you. It is not in the nature of an emergency, so I would like to speak with you at the houseboat. Would you both meet me there?"

Harris squinted for a moment at the phone. "Sure. An hour is good. Rush hour is subsiding, so we can get across town without too much trouble. Mele is just finishing some work, but that's not an issue. Why the houseboat?"

"I can explain when I see you there."

"Sure." Harris clicked to hang up, paused and turned to see his wife at the entrance from her home office. "Mele, get your coat. I'll let Bromo out." He didn't wait for the reply.

Slowing to a stop at the base of the sloping gravel road that served as Jake's driveway, Mele noticed first that Martik's car was already parked. In fact, he stood on the deck of Jake's boat, lifting his hand to offer a slight wave to the couple as they walked carefully down the old dock. Martik, his small notebook always at the ready, broke the nervous silence.

"Mrs. Daniels," he nodded slightly, "Mr. Daniels – I received a phone call late this afternoon from your son."

Harris gripped the hand of his wife. "Is he all right? Is he coming home?"

Seeing the smallest of trembling, Martik, reached out and placed his hand softly on her shoulder. "Yes, he seems to be all right. No, I don't think he has any immediate plans of returning. But let me tell you everything I know – and if anything comes to mind for you to add, please interrupt to tell me. That's our understanding – right?"

They both nodded.

"Jake told me on the phone that he was actually working with Luc Benoit and a French division of the FBI to uncover an art thief." Martik paused and observed as the couple looked at each other – clearly not understanding. "He told me that Luc had left something with him when they met here – a painting. And that I needed to find it." Again Martik paused as they took in the information. "So, I don't have any details to tell you, but I have to ask you, however – does this sound like your son, or does it seem as if he's hiding something? Also, and most importantly, has he been in touch with you?"

Mele spoke first. "No, Jake has not been in contact with us. As for your other questions, I don't think I can answer. There's nothing in what you said that couldn't have come from him."

"Okay the. Look, I'll be honest. I could get a search warrant for this boat, but I'm not sure how public I want to make this just yet. That is one reason I wanted you to join me here. Jake said that a painting was hidden behind a wall panel. He said I should get it and he said I should make it public that I have it."

The couple looked again at each other. Harris said, "If there's a wall panel, it will be in the cabin." He walked to the cabin entrance. "Probably that back wall, since the others are still in disrepair. However, this boat is Jake's passion and I don't want it damaged any more than it already is. Let me pull the proper tools to do this right." Harris walked to the stern of the craft and opened a large wooden toolbox on the deck.

"So this is Jake's passion?" Martik asked Mele.

"Oh, most definitely! This looks pretty damaged, but he absolutely lives to work on this in his spare time."

Martik looked around. All his spare time working? That IS dedication."

"Well, just between you and me, I think he believes that, if he can restore this, then he can restore himself. Does that sound crazy? Also, he claims that working here calms him – like a kind of meditation."

"You know, that actually makes pretty good sense." He looked around at the craft, nodding as if seeing it for the first time. "Not crazy at all.," he said to himself.

Harris returned with a large crowbar with a hard rubber sleeve for the prying end. He also had a long rod, also of metal coated with hard rubber. He walked to the back wall of the cabin, followed by Martik and Mele, and they began knocking and pushing on the wooden interior panels of the wall. "Here," Harris reported, pushing a panel to the side to expose the space between the interior and exterior walls of the houseboat. "That was certainly easier than I thought it would be."

"One moment," Martik said quickly. He pulled latex gloves from his jacket pocket, put them on, and reached for the rectangular wooden crate. Removing it carefully and setting in on the work table in the other corner of the cabin, he looked closely at the taped package. "Do you know what this is?"

"It certainly looks like a crate built for transporting a canvas," Harris added. "Are you going to open it?"

Martik paused to consider, then nodded and looking around the cabin, reached for a screwdriver from a gray toolbox on the floor. "Any secret to opening this sort of thing?"

Harris stepped forward and reached for the screwdriver, but not before Martik grabbed his wrist and, digging into his jacket pocket, handed him another pair of gloves. "You need to wear these. This is evidence from one aspect of a crime scene, and there are protocols."

Harris nodded, pulled on the gloves, and took the screwdriver. "You just need to be careful not to poke too vigorously, or the screwdriver can scrape the surface of whatever is inside. Then you have to work around the edges of the crate, prying slightly around – perhaps even a second time – to remove the top of the packing crate." He looked up at Martik and smiled slightly. "We have protocols as well."

Harris worked his way around the crate a second time, finally feeling the give of the top slats. He lifted the top to reveal a bubble-wrap. They lifted the painting

from the crate, set the wood aside, and Harris held the painting as Martik carefully removed the wrap. The painting now revealed, they set it on the table.

Mele looked over Harris' shoulder, then to her husband. They exchanged a questioning glance.

Martik looked from one to the other. "What is it? Why that reaction? Is this a valuable painting?"

Harris stepped back and pursed his lips. "No," he said, shaking his head. "Not at all."

"Then what am I looking at?"

"You're looking at an effort to copy the style of the Impressionists – but not a particularly good one."

"Are you sure of that?"

"Couldn't be more sure. The paint, particularly the blue, is a modern formulation. Also, lean over and have a sniff."

Martik leaned over, inhaled deeply, and looked back at Harris.

"Notice the slightly burnt smell? That is baked oil. Young painters will bake their paintings to dry the paint. Actual oil paint takes years to dry – decades to dry completely. You can speed up the process by baking, however."

"So this is a forgery?"

"Not at all. You can find a hundred of this ilk at any city art gallery – at least the low-rent galleries. Something you might expect from a MICA undergrad." Harris turned to his wife. "Sorry, Mele, didn't intend to slam your students."

Mele shrugged. "My students are sculptors. However, I have to agree with my husband's assessment, detective."

Martik leaned back. "Any idea why your son would want me to make known that I have this in my possession?"

"Can you call him, detective? Can we?"

"Sorry, no. The call came from a blanked number. If he's working with the FBI in France, that would be the case."

Mele raised a finger. "Unless he believed there was something else in this crate. That might make more sense."

Harris looked over, his head tilted. "So that someone made a switch between the time he left the country and now?"

Martik nodded. "At least between the time he saw you and today, to be more specific. Yes, that would fit the situation – whatever it is. So I'm guessing the best play would be to indicate publicly that we have recovered a painting, and leave it vague. Tell me, could Jake have been fooled and thought this was valuable?"

Harris shook his head. "Jake is a highly-regarded conservator. There is no way he thought this was any good."

Chapter 27

The ding of Jake's phone alarm was entirely unnecessary. Wide awake and in thought, he had forgotten that he had set it the night before, and quickly moved to silence it. Across the room, Lily stirred, rolled to her left, and slowly sat up in bed, lowering her head and rubbing behind her neck, her long curls undone and unleased in luxurious chaos. She, like Jake, had slept in clothes from the day before, yet she somehow looked more together that he either looked or felt.

"Good morning."

"Mmm. You've been up, I gather. And do I smell coffee?"

They had checked in to the small hotel on Limburgstraat the night before, and decided, feeling the whine of paranoia, that to register as a couple rather than take two rooms would arouse less suspicion in case they were being followed. The fact that the room had two double beds made the decision seem simpler. However, the familiarity of Lily's voice and the comfort of the setting made Jake wonder if it had been the best decision.

"Yes. Been up for a few hours, actually. The hotel's breakfast nook was set up early and I just got back with something to eat." He waved to a small round table on which he had set two croissants, packets of butter and jam, a hearty slice of cheese, and three cups of coffee – one of which he had already consumed.

Lily stood and stretched, pulling her hair back behind her head in a motion from which Jake could not look away. She walked to the table and sat in a chair, pulling the end off of one of the croissants. "So I gather you didn't sleep well. How are you feeling?"

Jake paused to consider. "Feeling used, actually." He let the statement hang in the air.

Lily tilted her head and looked at Jake. then she set her croissant back on the plate and reached for one of the coffee cups -- pulling off the cap and taking a small sip. "I know what you mean. I'm feeling a bit used myself."

Jake nodded and adjusted himself in the chair. "So Luc comes to me in Baltimore - out of the blue - after five years without contact. He wants me to guard this painting. My first inclination is not to believe a thing he tells me."

"Yes," Lily whispered, looking at her coffee. "Especially knowing Luc's history."

"But then, as we get into this whole mess, it starts to look like he wants to do something right - and is just in way over his head."

"Yes," Lily added, "Also knowing Luc's history."

"But now I'm in possession of a stolen painting, I've become aware of a forgery at the d'Orsay, I've been attacked, kidnapped, and have actually killed someone - although I admit I have no regrets about that part."

Jake waited for Lily to add a comment, but she didn't. "Now I'm here at Ghent with you, and Luc is actually working with an agent who is your husband."

Lily shifted in her chair. "So do we need to have that talk?"

"Maybe, but not until I ask you a question. And it's going to sound like a very ugly question." Jake waited.

Lily said nothing, but looked intently at Jake.

"The question is this: Do you trust your husband? Do the two of you have any secrets?" Jake saw the expression freeze on Lily's face. "I'm asking because something here isn't right. You know that as well as I do."

The expression on Lily's face softened. "You're right. There's something missing here - either we're being played or we're missing something big. However, you should know I trust Jean with my life, if it comes to that." Lily paused and added, "He's already saved my life, in fact."

Jake set down his coffee cup and leaned toward Lily.

"When you left," Lily breathed deeply, "you didn't know. I tried to tell you, but you weren't answering phone calls or e-mails."

Jake's throat was suddenly dry. "Didn't know what?"

Lily looked up, tears filling her eyes. "I was pregnant." The last syllable came out in a choked whisper."

Jake's mouth hung slack. "Pregnant? You had a—"

Lilly waved him off quickly. "No. I miscarried." She sniffed and looked down to collect herself. "It happens. But the point is, I was completely alone. You were gone, and Luc couldn't really handle it – although I give him points for trying. But I had been partnering with Jean, and he stepped up." Lily looked directly at Jake. "He saved me."

"Lily, I—" Jake shook his head slowly. "I'm so sorry. "I had no—"

"'No idea. Yes, I realize that." Lily paused and took a deep breath. "Look. I know you're sorry. I get that you feel guilty. But that was five years ago. We don't need to add your guilt to the mess we're in already. So I said it, it's out there, and that's that."

Jake looked down at his coffee cup, buried in thoughts.

"Come on. Finish your coffee," Lily said. We can talk more later if you want, but we've got work to do." She broke off a piece of the cheese. "Good coffee, by the way. Thanks."

Jake looked up and nodded, revealing a half-smile of admiration, and determined not to reveal the questions and the suspicions which still tugged at him.

Lily smiled in return. "Now let's get the day organized before we leave." She broke off one of the ends of a croissant and nibbled.

Jake nodded toward the plate on the table. "So are you still planning to eat the ends off both of the croissants and save me the middles?"

"That was my plan," Lily replied, reaching for the plate.

"Still goes to voice mail," Lily said, putting her phone into the pocket of her slacks. Showered and refreshed, they had walked to meet Luc at the café he described – not seeing him there at 8:00 nor again at 8:15.

"Would Jean have his phone off if he were involved in something? Is there a good reason he's not picking up? What are your instincts telling you?" Jake looked once again at the café as they rounded the corner. "One more loop around the block, and by then Bavo's will be open and we can just go in."

Lily said nothing as she lowered her hand into her pocket to feel for her phone.

Ten silent minutes of walking found them in the short line to enter St. Bavo's Cathedral. As they entered, Jake leaned over toward Lily. "Most tourists think the altarpiece will be in the center of the cathedral, behind the choir, but it's actually just off to our left in one of the chapels." They turned, following a smaller group of tourists.

"Oh my," Lily whispered as they turned left a second time. Jake stared, scanning the magnificent panels and moving closer to the restraining chord for a better look.

The Ghent Altarpiece, also referred to as The Adoration of the Mystic Lamb, was unfolded before them. The thick bullet-proof glass had been temporarily removed for cleaning, so extra guards were on duty. The unfolded display meant that the panels which formed the outer view were not visible. The altarpiece was formed in three sections – an inner section of four panels and two wings of four panels each. The total view was an astounding eleven feet high and fifteen feet wide. When folded, the inner panels would be hidden and twelve outer panels would then be visible. Seeing the unfolded view, however, was the goal of every art lover and informed tourist to Ghent. Before them, in vivid colors painted on oak panels six hundred years old, were scenes of such immaculate detail that it was difficult to see these as merely paint on wood rather than scenes of vivid life. The lower central panel was the longest and showed massive crowds of spectators come to adore the Sacred Lamb. Each face in the multitude was as unique as it was detailed, no matter how far into the background of the scene. In the second level above this wide central panel were three vertical panels. God the Father occupied the center in glorious red and gold, flanked by Mary on the left and John the Baptist on the right. This central collection of four panels was hinged to two wings. Each wing with two levels and two panels on each level – four panels on each wing.

Everywhere they looked, their eyes rested on some new wonder, some impossible detail, some incredible color. The small crowd in the chapel murmured in reverential whisper – several languages all expressing the wonder of, "How did he do this?"

"I can't believe I never thought to come here and see this before now. It is—" Jake fought for words, "— incredible."

"Completely," Lily added quietly. "But as wonderful as it is, why are we here? What did Luc want us to see?"

Jake walked over to the panels on the left wing and motioned Lily to join him. "I think I'm getting it." He pointed to the lower panel on the far left. "That's the Just Judges panel, right? That's the panel that Van der Veken copied, and here's the notation." He pointed to a small white plaque below the panel, printed in both French and English, stating that the panel was a reproduction of the original.

"Yes, and Van der Veken was an expert with van Eyck's style. See the tower in the distance? Most painters would make sure the lines were accurate, but would assume a viewer's attention was to the events of the foreground. Not van Eyck. I'm sure you could count the windows in the tower – and if one of those windows needed washing – he would find a way to include the smudge on the glass. Veken did his best, but copying a van Eyck is a tall order."

Jake nodded, thinking. "So Veken copied this from photographs of the original? That's the story, right?"

"Yes," Lily said. "He collected several photographs and combined that with his expertise and understanding of van Eyck."

"Photographs from the late 1920's or early 1930's, right?"

"Yes, that makes sense I guess."

"So those would be black-and-white photographs, since color photos of that time would have poorer definition than black-and-white."

"If you say so."

Jake said nothing for several seconds, looking carefully at the men on horseback – somber and moving methodically to the right. Their movement seeming to bump into the similar procession of knights on horseback in the next panel. Even the background terrain and foliage seemed to indicate the two panels could be viewed as one scene, split vertically. A prominent plateau in the background of one continuing into the background of the other. Lighting and shadow were equally consistent and flawless.

Lily turned to look at him. "What is it?"

Jake returned Lily's glance. "Pretty good fake, wouldn't you say?"

"Very good. What's your point?"

He shook his head. "I don't know. It just seems awfully good – and considering the circumstances, maybe too good."

Suddenly, a hand touched Jake's shoulder and he immediately felt his fist clench and his arm tighten, fighting the instinct to raise his elbow and turn sharply to his right – catching whomever was unlucky enough to be in the path of his swing. Turning, he saw Luc standing, leaning back in response to Jake's aggressive move.

"Whoa, my friend. I do apologize for not arriving on time, but I'm glad to see you both well and in front of this masterwork."

"Where's Jean?" Lily said, before Luc had even finished his sentence.

"No worry, Jean is well. He's lingering back a bit to make sure we weren't followed here. Come over this way." Luc walked to the right side of the altarpiece.

"About the Just Judges," Jake interrupted. "I've got a few questions."

"No no no. This isn't about that at all." Luc replied, pulling them to the side and pointing up to the panel on the top level, depicting Eve. "It is about her. It has always been about her. Clear your mind of anything else and look closely at her."

The second level of panels centered on a striking personification of God, flanked by Mary on the left and John the Baptist on the right. These three formed the center section, with the hinged wings to either side. Left of Mary were angels singing, and to the right of John the Baptist were angels playing instruments. These were the Musical Angels panels. Farthest to the left was the image of Adam – looking somber and ashamed, holding leaves to cover his genitals. Farthest to the right was Eve. He turned to Luc. "Yea. And?"

"No. Study it. Look closely. Then we need to leave so that I can tell you more."

Lily pursed her lips, but turned to also look carefully at the panel. Eve stood, also somber and ashamed, although perhaps a bit more contemplative than Adam – showing a high forehead and tousled brown hair. Her belly protruded, creating a pear-shaped figure that, although not particularly attractive by modern standards, nonetheless revealed a fascinating mixture of innocence and promised sexuality. She did not hold an apple, as might be expected, but rather a stranger lumpy fruit, its slightly orange tint indicating a citrus. Lily tilted her head and peered up to examine the strange object more closely.

"Citrus medica," Luc said, noticing her stare. "Probably a citron – a citrus fruit with its origins in south Asia and the middle east." He reached to touch both Jake and Lily. "Come, we need to leave now. Back to the café, but at an inside table, I think is best. When we leave the cathedral, you two turn to the left and I'll turn to the right. We'll each go around the cathedral to the café at the rear."

"Is that really necessary?" Jake said, not bothering to hide his irritation.

"Probably not necessary. However, a simple enough precaution, I think."

In less than a minute, all three gathered around a table in the back corner of the café, even though most of the patrons had selected tables out in the early morning sun.

"Jake – for you, first things first. I think I know why the Collector—"

"Wilson," Jake interrupted. "Call him Wilson. Enough of the comic book shit."

"Okay. Why Wilson wants you so badly. It isn't to copy something. There are other qualified forgers around – especially if the piece is an Impressionist work." Luc turned to Lily. "Those are incredibly easy to forge. A bit of chemistry and a bit of talent. It is jokingly said that Monet painted approximately 2500 paintings, and over 4000 of them are owned by collectors and museums." Luc paused for a reaction to his humor, but getting nothing, continued. "When I was escaping from Romigny, not too long after you, I broke into a small locked closet at the studio. It had always been open and empty when I was working there. But now it wasn't. There's a painting there – on a wood panel – and you have just seen it."

"What are you talking about?" Jake shifted in his seat, his irritation near boiling over.

"Eve. You saw the panel of Eve in the altarpiece. Well so did I. I swear to you they are, as far as I can see, identical. However, the panel at the studio is broken in two. The wood has dried, I expect." Luc paused and looked intently at Jake.

"And?"

"And I think the Coll—Wilson wants you to repair it for him. He wants someone who can copy and someone who can repair. Your reputation as a conservator is greater than you think."

"What's the point? The Eve panel is here."

"The point is this. In a few months, the entire altarpiece will be moved to Brussels for an exhibition of Dutch masters. The moving process always creates security risks, and I think Wilson intends on making a switch."

"Like his father did with the Just Judges?"

Luc looked quickly at Jake, wide-eyed, and then shook his head. "No, no. This is not about that. You need to forget about that and focus on the real situation."

Jake looked to Lily. "Doesn't the FBI have enough on this guy? What are we possibly going to add to what's already known about him?"

"I can answer that question." Everyone turned immediately to the voice walking toward them.

"Jean!" Lily said exhaling and standing. "Where have you been? Are you okay? I tried to call—"

"I know you did." Jean looked briefly over his shoulder and pulled a chair to the table. "I couldn't use my phone." He reached over to take Lily's hand and looked around the table. "We have almost nothing on Wilson – at least nothing that would complement his arrest. His hired men will say nothing. Luc is correct. We need to do something. If we could locate his stolen artworks – well-- That was supposed to be Luc's role, but his disloyalty was uncovered."

"And I was nearly there. Everything was on my laptop and also on my tablet. However, now both of them have been stolen."

Jake spoke without looking up. "So what you need is either a location of stolen art or your laptop or your tablet – any one of the three. Is that what I'm hearing? Any of those three options will work?"

"Yes. The files on my laptop and tablet are well hidden. I don't think anyone has been able to destroy or even find them."

"Unless the laptop and tablet were themselves destroyed." Jake continued to look down.

There were a few seconds of silence around the table. Jake took a deep breath and looked up. "I guess we all know what comes next. Jean, Luc, we need to find a way to stay in touch. Then, Jean, get Lily away from here. I need to make one last call, then I need to get back to Romigny. It seems as if I'll be going to work for Wilson. Pardon me, 'The Collector'."

Lily looked over at Jake, her eyebrows angled in anger. "I am not helpless here, and I don't intend to be treated as if I was!"

Jean put his hand on her shoulder. "No one considers you helpless – least of all me. We have plenty of work to do at our end. But Jake is correct. You need to be out of sight, or you become a target and a bargaining chip."

Jake looked at Lily. "Jean's right. And Wilson already seems to be holding all of the chips."

Chapter 28

It took Detective Martik 27 minutes to cut through the thick walls of traffic trying to maneuver around downtown Baltimore in the morning rush to reach the Daniels' residence on Park Ave. Moving east to west was notoriously the worst, as half of the cross streets were impaired by roadwork and the other half equally impaired by the lack of roadwork. As he finally pulled to the curb, he exited quickly, almost – but not quite – forgetting to button his jacket. Harris Daniels was already at the door.

"Thank you for coming and please come in. We have some news."

Martik reflexively reached into his pocket for his small notebook as he walked past Harris, who held the door. "Sorry it took so long. Cross-town traffic. And as you didn't suggest an emergency, I didn't use lights or siren. I think a lower profile is better."

"No explanations necessary," Mele replied, entering from the back room. "We'll get right to the point. Jake just contacted us."

Martik paused, opened his notebook, and when Harris pointed to the chair, he sat. Mele sat on the sofa and Harris disappeared into the back room. "So, yes, he called us. Before we were able to say anything, he said he was in France, driving to someplace in Romigny. It's a small town outside of Riems." Noting Martik's blank response, she added, "R-i-e-m-s. Northeast of Paris, about halfway to the Belgian border." Martik wrote in his notebook and she continued. "He said that everyone was all right, and he hoped it would all be over soon - although he didn't say what it was that would be over. He also apologized for not calling sooner, but said that he didn't want our phone number in his call history in case his phone was taken. He said he was calling from a throw-away phone." Mele paused. "He seemed very calm, very matter-of-fact. But I don't know what he's involved with."

Martik shrugged in reply. "Did you tell him about the painting, Mrs. Daniels?"

Harris entered the room with three mugs of coffee, setting the tray on the low table in front of the sofa. Martik reached for a mug. "If this is all over soon, as he suggests, I confess I will miss your coffee."

"So I told him about the cheap painting in the crate, detective," Harris added, taking one of the mugs for himself and sitting on the sofa next to his wife. "That seemed to throw him off a bit. He asked me to repeat what I had said a second time, and I told him a high school art student could have completed it. It was a few seconds before he replied. He asked if you had made it clear that you had a stolen painting in your possession, and I said it had been on the local news - albeit not exactly a headline story."

Martik sipped, thinking. "So he wanted me to make this clear because he was afraid someone would come for you both - on the assumption you had it."

"But it's little more than trash," Harris said.

"Yes. And that's not good." Mele looked up, about to speak. "Jake didn't realize it, which suggests that there is something going on here that he doesn't know about."

"I agree, detective," Harris added.

Martik paused. "Anything else?"

"Yes," Mele said. "Jake wants us to leave the area for a while."

Martik looked up, eyebrows raised. "That is definitely a good idea."

"Do you really think there is some imminent danger, detective?"

"I don't exactly know what to think. But Jake seemed surprised that this painting is a fake – even though you are sure that he would have known it immediately."

"Immediately. Yes," Harris said.

"That means something is happening in Baltimore that your son was not aware of. Someone switched that painting, after your son hid it. That means someone knew where he had it hidden, since the houseboat didn't seem damaged in any way. And that someone also knew what the painting was, or he or she would not have known to replace it with a Pissarro. Whatever is going on here in Baltimore, it is STILL going on.. I agree with Jake's assessment, and I do think it best that you find somewhere to go for a short while."

Mele set her mug down quickly, spilling some coffee onto the tray. "Well I don't agree. I have my classes, Harris has work to do, and I don't fancy running someplace for who knows how long. We are going to see this through right here. Besides, whoever switched the painting realizes we don't have it – because he or she does!"

Harris reached over to take her hand, smiled at her and looked over to Martik. "You heard the lady. Sorry, but we're staying."

Martik fought to hide his smile. "I don't agree with you, but I do respect your decision, and you may be right about the switch. Still, I'll do my best to double-check on your safety. I already have your street on frequent patrols, and I'll position someone unmarked when I can, but you have to promise to call immediately if anything looks suspicious."

"We will, and thank you." Mele added, "Anyway, that was the gist of the phone call. He told us to be careful and that he would have to go."

Martik stood, taking one last sip of coffee and placing his notebook in his pocket. "I don't suppose there was a call-back number?" They both shook their heads. He paused, then added, "Did he say anything about Ms. Nicole - or O'Donnell?" They shook their heads a second time. "Okay. Keep a low profile, keep on alert for anything out of the ordinary – particularly people who don't seem to know the neighborhood – and stay in touch. Promise me."

"Promise," Mele said. Harris nodded.

Martik stood and closed his pocket notebook. "I'll go back to the station and go over the patrol rosters." He turned to look at the couple as he left. "So we are clear on the plan?"

"Clear," Harris said. As he closed the door behind Martik, he turned to Mele. "Yes, a plan. We need one of our own. Just in case."

Mele nodded. "I have a bit of an idea."

Chapter 29

As Jake pulled into the gravel parking area in front of the gray cement-block building, he saw the two guards at the door, like before, rise from their relaxed positions and stand ready, one immediately calling on his white cell phone. In the hours driving back from Ghent, Jake had run this scenario over and over, from every perspective. His plan was based on posturing – predicated on it, in fact – so he had driven the last few kilometers getting "in character."

Stepping out of the car and closing the door loudly, he walked toward the two men, trying to look relaxed and confident, calling out as he approached. "The Collector said he would meet me here. Is he here?"

The two looked at each other and said nothing. One pulled his gun.

In response, as he had planned on his drive back to this place, Jake took that opportunity to pull his gun also, although he didn't aim it forward, but rather let his arm hang down from his side. "Here we go," he mumbled to himself. The second guard lifted a gun from his back and both took a step forward – almost in unison as if some practiced choreography of intimidation. It was the sort of reaction Jake had been hoping for: intimidation, but without action.

"Quit the theatrics," Jake announced, walking toward them and stopping a few feet from the pair. Two guns were in the air pointing at Jake, and his hung loose at his side. One of the men nodded to Jake's gun and motioned for him to hand it over.

Noting the gesture and attempting a grin, Jake said, "Sure thing. But let's get this straight. You aren't going to shoot me, since you haven't yet - even though I'm standing here with a gun at my side. In fact, you have been told specifically not to shoot me. So I'm guessing I'm untouchable."

"Nobody's untouchable," one of the guards growled in response, a timbre in his voice hinting of British background.

Jake shrugged, lifted his gun, and shot the man in the foot. The guard went down with a yell, and groaned as he clutched at his shoe. The other guard's face twisted in hatred, and he breathed deeply and quickly, but did nothing. "See how it is? Back in Paris I used to be 'a guy,' but now I'm 'THE guy'. See how it is?" Jake handed his gun to the guard still standing and walked forward into the building, not looking back and making sure they did not see the sweat beading on his forehead. Once inside, he walked to the chair still positioned beside the single desk in the building, and sat. His pulse beginning to slow from the tachycardiac rush of the scene outside.

The phone rang.

Jake did not move as the phone continued to ring. After the fifth ring, it stopped. Jake stayed in the chair and waited.

After perhaps a half minute, by Jake's reckoning, the door at the rear opened and a man stepped inside. An imposing figure, he seemed to stand at just over six feet and carried a girth worth considering, perhaps close to 300 pounds – maybe more forgivingly somewhere around 270. As he stepped closer, however, Jake noticed the features of age in his face and on his hands. He was dressed in a gray suit with a checked vest – clearly expensive, yet hopelessly out of fashion and out of date. The man stopped a dozen feet from the desk. "What made you think I would actually be here?" The voice was deep, with the internal echo of a practiced base, and he spoke slowly, seeming to consider each word. There also seemed to be a smile that wanted a foothold on the big man's face but could not find one.

Jake shifted, staying in the chair. "Simple. You need to show me something. Something complicated enough that you need me to see it first-hand – therefore too complicated to leave to a subordinate who might get the details wrong. So, yea, I knew you would be here."

"Tell me, why did you return here, Jacob Daniels? Why the change of heart?"

"No change of heart. Lily is now safe, and I would like this thing over – and I would like my life back."

"You aren't concerned for your parents back in Baltimore?"

"They're away."

"And if I told you they were already found?"

Jake swallowed, but refused to take the bait. "If you told me that, I wouldn't believe you – so let's get on with this. What do I have to do?"

The Collector considered the question and the confidence of this adversary, and decided to treat both lightly. He chuckled humorlessly. "I have a job for which you are uniquely qualified."

"The Eve panel." Jake looked to gauge the man's response, however there was no reaction he could discern.

"So," he began after a silence following Jake's statement. "You have just informed me from your response that Lucas Benoit is still alive. I had suspected as much. People don't escape from me, and you have managed it twice. I suspected you had help from someone, and now I see." He chuckled again as he turned and began to walk to the rear of the building. "I suppose that is why I have not heard from my man in Baltimore. Ah well. Come. Follow me."

Wilson stopped at a door along one wall, near the rear and not far from the room where Lily had been held earlier. He pulled a set of keys, and then noticed that the door was not locked. He smiled and shook his head. "I have been careless," he said without turning. "I will have to stop underestimating you, Mr. Daniels." He opened the door, and removed the top of the Eve panel and the bottom third which had broken off. Finally, still with disregard, he turned to Jake. "So I probably don't have to say any more. You seem to know what this is and what you have to do."

"*Have* to do?"

"For your liberty. And the liberty of your parents, of course – assuming the Pissarro is also returned."

Jake walked over to examine the panel pieces. He fought to control his expression as he organized what he knew, what he had just learned, and what conclusions seemed likely. "You want this repaired?"

"Of course."

"And you want it to look good enough for you to exchange with the original?"

Wilson shrugged. "Indeed."

"And you need this before the Sacred Lamb goes out for exhibition?"

Wilson stiffened slightly. "Enough. Just do it." There was a sudden impatience in his voice.

Jake stepped back and looked directly at Wilson. "You know that isn't possible. Not without a compositional examination of the paints, the varnish, and most importantly the wood. Do you have a gas chromatograph mass spectrometer here anyplace?" Jake pretended to look around the building and shrugged his shoulders. "You are even likely going to need a DNA test of the wood. Van Eyck didn't use oak panels from the area – it had already been effectively deforested. He purchased panels from Poland. Any examiner will find the difference." Once again, Jake waited to assess Wilson's reaction.

Wilson's scowl was beginning to encompass his demeanor. "I know that! This panel is from Polish oak. Further, I'll give you the spectrometer analysis, and we won't need a DNA test because you are going to make this so good no one will be suspicious. Am I being clear?"

Jake nodded and considered what he was about to say. He decided that saying it was worth the risk of being shot on the spot. "Okay. That's clear. However, I'll have to see the other two panels." He looked Wilson in the eyes and measured his response.

Wilson's chin lifted and he looked down at Jake. "What other panels?" Jake could see that the question was not a serious one, but meant to assess what Jake already knew.

"The Just Judges, of course. This Eve panel is clearly van der Veken's work. Apparently, he was more productive than anyone realized."

"I should warn you, Mr. Daniels, about being too smart for your own good. I try not to be a violent man, but I can be quite vindictive when I'm pushed."

Jake raised his hands in supplication. "Nevertheless, I do need to see that panel. At least if you want this done properly." Jake's pulse had quickened when Wilson did not react to his initial use of the plural, 'panels,' and although he had pivoted to the mention of only one, his pulse had not yet slowed. He had a hunch that there was even more to this than anyone had yet said – perhaps more than Luc knew himself. And his deliberate use of the plural was meant to add some mass to that hunch. The puzzle pieces were starting to form a larger picture.

"I will leave you to make your initial assessment," Wilson said, turning toward the back door. A tall, well-dressed man with short-cropped black hair and a thin mustache appeared from the back room. "My associate will answer any preliminary questions you may have, and I'll make the arrangements you just requested. I will be back within the hour." Without looking back, he left.

A silence followed as Jake watched Wilson leave, and as the tall man watched Jake with the same intensity. "Okay, associate. Your boss – The Collector," Jake added in a mock deep voice, "said there was a spectrometer analysis on this. Could I see that?" He bent over the panel as the man walked to the back room.

After a minute, the man returned. "I don't see anything. What does it look like?"

Jake tilted his head as he considered the man. "Well it will be a stack of papers, some of which will have thin line graphs, and some will have small numbers lined up in columns. Or else it's a computer file that hasn't been printed yet."

The man returned to the back room as Jake turned to admire the accuracy and the detail van der Veken had put into the copy of the Eve panel. "Seriously gifted forger," Jake said to himself.

After another minute the man returned. "I saw no papers anything like you describe. Perhaps the file is on this?" Jake tried not to betray his surprise as the man handed him a tablet.

"Do you have the password?" Jake asked as he clicked open the tablet, fighting for control of his hand, which had begun to tremble. The man shrugged and Jake, thinking for a moment, entered Luc's old computer password. The tablet came to life. The man turned and walked to the back as Jake pulled out his phone and repositioned the larger portion of the Eve panel. "The Collector is pulling up. You still need a password?

Jake looked up. "No," Jake said to the man, "I got what I needed. Just got lucky."

Chapter 30

The two men stopped on Park Avenue in Baltimore one house down from their target. The idea was not to be immediately associated with the address given them, in case anyone was looking – as they expected would be the case. Not that such initial discovery mattered much to either of them. This was an older couple and a simple job. Get in, rough things up to whatever extent was required, get the painting and exit. They were aware of the news report that the painting had been taken by the police and was protected elsewhere, but they also had been given good reason not to believe the news report. They had never met their employer in person, but nonetheless he had assured them that either the painting was on the premises or the couple would know where to obtain it.

Simple job. Quick and simple.

They stepped up to the green double-door and rang the bell. When no one responded the two men looked at each other, shrugged, and, in choreographed unison, kicked the double door at the point where the two halves met at one central door knob. A handsome, stately door – yet the two halves meeting in the center created an obvious weak point. One kick to each side and the door crackled and snapped – folding inward.

Both men landed solidly on both feet, finishing as if well-rehearsed. They stared in through the pieces of the shattered doorway at an older man who stood motionless, cell phone poised in his right hand. One of the men kicked again, upward at the man's hand, sending the cell phone to the floor where the second man stomped on it – finishing their entrance into the Daniels home without yet speaking a word.

"Just step back," one of the men said, breaking the momentary silence, "and we can get this done and you won't have anything broken but the door."

Harris stepped back inside, glancing as he turned to make sure Mele wasn't visible. The two men didn't display any weapons, but Harris noted one had his hand tucked behind his back, under a light jacket, and he reflexively raised his hands slightly as he backed into the living room. "What do you want?" Harris said, hopefully loudly enough for Mele to hear and react.

"We want the painting. Just that, old man. Just the painting." Harris caught the thickened tone and elongated vowels of South Baltimore, suggesting these were two local hires.

"What painting? Harris waved to the walls of the home. "These are mostly just student works. I don't see what you—"

The man with his hand tucked behind his jacket stepped forward and stopped less than an inch from Harris' face. Harris froze, mouth still open in mid-sentence. "Better stop fucking around, old man." He began to pull his hand from under his jacket.

"Anybody want some coffee? Do I hear guests?" Mele walked in from the kitchen, two mugs of coffee in her hands and clearly squinting through nearly shut eyes.

"Just - just a salesman, dear." Harris looked at the intruders and motioned with his hand over his face that his wife couldn't see well. "You need to get your glasses, love."

Mele took two hesitant steps forward and with one motion, tossed two mugs of hot coffee into the faces of the two intruders. "Bromo!" she yelled.

A brown and white streak with black trim over a muzzle flashing fangs and barking wildly bounded into the room, one-hopped over the sofa and was on the man closest to Harris. The man was flailing wildly to keep the dog away, but Bromo had bitten hard into the man's arm, and was not about to be flung away. He pulled and yanked at the arm, which was now bleeding profusely under the shirt, the dog frenzied as if it was a marvelous new toy that needed breaking in. The man squirmed to the side and managed to roll free. He reached for the gun, which was now lying on the carpet in front of the sofa, but Harris stomped down as hard as he could on the torn and bloodied arm. The man shrieked and Bromo was on him again, this time going for the other arm, which had flung out to the side and presented the most convenient target for the dog.

The second intruder struggled to his feet, still wiping scalding coffee from his face and squinting to regain his vision. Moving surprisingly fast, he was on Harris, pulling a knife from his jacket and reaching to grab his throat. There was a metallic clang, and the man's eyes rolled back and he slumped to the floor. Mele picked up the knife and set it on the coffee table, shaking her head slowly as she examined the broken casting of one of August Rodin's sculptured hands.

Harris, breathing heavily, was standing on top of the first man, one leg on each arm. The man moaned and tried weakly to move, but could not escape Bromo's growling muzzle, hot breath and teeth – quivering with anticipation and dripping a mix of saliva and blood into the man's face.

Harris and Mele looked at each other as, in the distance, they heard the siren.

Chapter 31

Hearing the slight scuff of footsteps behind him, Jake crouched and picked up the smaller piece of the Eve panel, looking closely. He glanced up as Wilson stopped and stood over him. "Yes, I can do this - but I do need to see the Just Judges." He waited to see what emotion would greet his acknowledgement that he knew Wilson's secret - but he received only indifference.

"Yes, I will take you there now. Perhaps along the way you can tell me how you knew that I had the original in my collection." As before, his words were slow and enunciated as if each syllable was stressed.

"No great secret. You told me. I asked about seeing the original panel and you didn't object. That was it."

"But you asked about panels - with an 's'."

Jake shrugged. "Did I? Anyway, that's how I figured it out."

There was a pause, and then a half smile on Wilson's face. "An old trick, Mr. Daniels. I should have seen it coming."

Jake stood, holding the small piece of the Eve panel. "I'll need to take this along."

"As you like."

They walked silently to the back door and to a waiting black Megrane, similar to the one Jake had been taken in the day before. As before, the rear windows were blackened. This time, however,

Wilson's assistant held a cloth bag that he motioned to place over Jake's head.

"Really?" Jake said. I can't see out the windows anyway.

"Put it on, Mr. Daniels, or I shall have it tied on at the neck. Are we clear?"

Jake nodded and pulled the bag over his head. It smelled of disinfectant and was pulled together under his chin and fastened with a Velcro strip. He allowed himself to be escorted into the back of the car, which tilted slightly as Wilson got into the back seat next to him. As they pulled away, he had no idea what had become of the two guards in the front of the building. The wounded man had probably been taken somewhere for medical attention, but even if both were still there, Jake didn't think Luc and Jean would have much of a problem with them.

The ride seemed to be about half of an hour, during which Jake remained silent, despite a few questions from Wilson gauging how much he knew and how he had come by his information - probably trying to assess what level of threat was posed by the FBI. Jake, however, said nothing - also trying to assess how far he could push this man who had shown almost no affect so far. Wilson's violence, Jake was beginning to assume, was not a product of any sadistic tendency, but more of an indifference to what might or might not happen to anyone else.

The car dipped down an embankment and rolled to a stop. The diver opened the door and helped Jake from the back seat - the cooler air and concrete feel of the floor indicating an underground garage. When the bag was removed, he saw that he was indeed in a garage below some structure. Wilson turned and walked to a set of stairs at the rear wall of the garage, saying nothing but apparently expecting Jake to follow.

At the top of the stairs, Wilson entered a code into the lock of a steel door, which opened to a small landing and another steel door, with another coded lock. The second door opened to a room which seemed to emerge suddenly from another time. Lighting was low, and provided by two art nouveau table lamps and an impossibly ornate chandelier.

Everywhere Jake saw the luxury of another time. Furniture was tall, intricately upholstered, fringed with laced borders, and predominantly deep red in color. Walls sported dark wood below a chair rail, with wallpaper above. The wallpaper was a light blue with gold filigree.

Jake couldn't decide whether to sneer or to laugh at the absurdity of the decor - but chose to do neither. Without reacting to the nineteenth century bordello-chic nightmare around him, he strode to one wall highlighting a painting with a gold frame. A small lamp above the painting cast a soft light on the landscape. "Constable?" he asked as he approached. He knew it was, in fact, by the English landscapist John Constable, but was looking to impress Wilson.

"Why yes, it is. You have a good eye."

Jake looked closely at the painting. True, it was by Constable - but like every artist, not everything he painted was a masterpiece. This particular landscape was overly romantic, almost saccharine in tone, and revealed one corner where the brush strokes were rough. Jake assumed it was, in fact, unfinished, and that Constable probably discarded the work, recognizing it as a lost cause. He turned to Wilson, saying nothing but waiting.

Wilson stood, apparently waiting for some compliment of this first view of his collection, but after a moment nodded. "Yes, of course. Right this way." He walked to a dark mahogany door on one wall.

The next room was much more spare of decoration or furniture, with the exception of two wing-backed chairs back-to-back in the center of the room. It resembled many galleries in museums - devoid of much that would distract the viewer from the art. The walls were cream-colored and lighting was recessed in the ceiling. On three of the four walls, paintings were hung at eye-level, with enough variation in height to keep the room from looking too monotonous. There were interspersed small pedestals with works of sculpture or fine porcelain. Occasionally, artifacts hung on the walls among the paintings. The wall with the door, behind them, had no paintings. The spaces on each side of the door were taken by two large cylindrical columns of colored glass mosaic tiles - probably by Tiffany - or someone who worked in his studio.

"Impressive," Jake said, noting to himself that he actually meant it. He nodded his appreciation and looked over at Wilson, who appeared to be smiling at Jake's admiration. He walked slowly down the wall to his left, noting the array of artists' names and paused at a small penciled work on yellow-tinted paper. "Michelangelo? Really?"

Wilson stepped forward, beaming. "Yes, yes. Just a sketch, of course. Just a sketch," he added in false modesty.

Jake continued to the rear wall and stopped in the middle. There it hung - Van Eyck's glorious colors and meticulous attention to detail visible in every corner of the panel. "The Just Judges," he said quietly, as though speaking to the panel itself. "So here you are." He held up the portion of the Eve panel and looked at both. "You have to admire the technical abilities of Van der Veken," he said to Wilson. "He could have been a great artist in his own right."

"Perhaps. Water under the bridge, however," Wilson replied, regaining his emotionally neutral, carefully enunciated tone.

Jake noticed that the panel was placed with nothing immediately on either side. He pointed to the space on the right of the Just Judges and turned to Wilson. "Is this reserved for the Eve panel?"

"That is the intention, Mr. Daniels. And I have no doubt you will make that possible."

Jake nodded and took note of the equal space on the left of the Just Judges - confirming what he already suspected. Looking again to the right, following the room to the third wall, he stopped in front of a small painting - hoping that enough time had elapsed for the next part of the plan to unfold..

"That is my Corot," Wilson said. "It was the first piece of my collection."

Jake looked closely. "Yes, a Corot. But not a very good one."

Wilson paused, the smile evaporating. "Perhaps. But a Corot, just the same."

Jake turned to the man, who had seemed to swell in anticipation of an argument. "But that is the way with so many collectors of art. Museums, too, I'm afraid."

Wilson waited for him to continue, but lost patience. "What is the way?"

Jake decided to go for the push, to measure the tensile strength of Wilson's emotions. "Well, you imagine yourselves to be collectors of art - when in fact you're just autograph hunters."

Wilson stared, his face reddening.

"For example, this Corot. If it didn't have his name on it, you wouldn't give it a second look. It certainly isn't one of his best. And the Constable in the other room? I'm betting you've walked passed many better works in galleries that suffered only because they didn't have a recognized signature. No, I'm afraid you are a collector of autographs. Don't worry about it, though. Most museums suffer from the same weakness." Jake tried to appear calm, despite wondering if he had gone too far. "Don't get me wrong. There are some spectacular pieces here. But it's hit or miss, wouldn't you say? And is this the only room after - what is it - three generations of collecting?"

Jake had been watching the colors shift over Wilson's face, but then saw them fade with his last question.

Wilson pulled a ring with a few keys from his pocket. "I wonder why you are so interested in angering me," he said with his deliberate staccato enunciation.

Jake watched Wilson's face, but said nothing.

Wilson walked to a cabinet along the left wall, displaying several porcelain vases. He pulled and the cabinet rolled from the wall, revealing another door, which he unlocked. "Here. This may bring a respectful tone back to your voice."

A low light came on automatically as they entered the second room. Much larger than the first, it also sported a spiral staircase and a second balcony level of artworks, again with two wing-back chairs in the center of the room. Jake scanned the walls, He fought to keep his stance relaxed and his demeanor calm although he recognized some of the world's best-known works of art. Was that a study for El Greco's *Trinity*? One of the premier pieces from the Prado in Madrid? And Whistler's *Symphony in White*? How many times had he stood before that painting in the National Gallery? Had he been gazing at a fake all those years or was this the forgery? He found himself doubting not only what he saw, but what he had believed up to this point had been real. Elsewhere he saw pieces he did not recognize, but painted by artists universally revered. How many museums and private collectors were unaware that some of their pieces were little more than excellent forgeries – and that the originals could be found in this room. And how many stolen works were on display here, And there, on the back wall, was the work that Jake suspected had been in the collection since the closing days of World War II – a missing puzzle piece that now fit into place. And now, having seen it, Jake realized he had seen too much to be allowed to simply leave the employment of The Collector. At least not alive.

It was Van Eyck's John the Baptist panel. "So he's been here all the time?"

"Yes, he has. My father submitted one of Van der Vecken's best forgeries in its place and kept the original."

"But let me guess," Jake added. "Van der Vecken didn't have the right Polish oak for the Just Judges."

"No, not at the time. He found more later, from an antique bookcase, would you believe. Right age, right geography. But not until after the Just Judges switch had already been made." Wilson had walked to the center of the room and was staring at the John the Baptist panel. "And the wood from that bookcase was used for the Eve panel. Soon I will have three of the Ghent panels in my collection. How remarkable is that?" He spoke as if to himself.

"An unparalleled accomplishment, I have to admit," Jake said, seeing the small box set into the wall by the door and looking up to the ceiling His quick scan revealed only two cameras and recessed lighting fixtures. No sprinkler system, as he had suspected - and hoped. "It is amazing." Jake paused and looked directly at Wilson. "So can we agree that I am cooperating solely for the freedom of my family? I'm assuming my freedom and my life have been removed from the bargaining table I'm guessing that is the new arrangement now that I have seen this." Wilson looked back at him and waited. "So that means that my cooperation with you depends entirely on how well I can trust that you will leave them alone."

Wilson lifted the tilt of his head. "It seems you have come to understand the new limitations imposed by our current predicament. Perhaps I shouldn't have shown you this room. However, you taunted me, and now here we are. I'm truly sorry for your situation, but do this for me and I assure you your parents will remain unharmed." Wilson shrugged. "My apology, Mr. Daniels - but you do understand."

Jake nodded. "And the Pissarro? How will you get that back?"

Wilson inhaled deeply. "I suddenly find that I care little for the Pissarro. This has become much more significant." He continued speaking slowly as if considering every word before uttering it. "I will, of course, endeavor to have it returned to me. However, I will bring no harm to your mother or father in doing so. So regardless of whether I have that painting or not, your parents will be safe. I give you my word."

"Your word? Really?" Jake shook his head. "That's all I get?"

"Mr. Daniels," Wilson's voice rose to a baritone roar. "I just gave you my word.. No one questions my word!" He paused, breathing heavily. "No one!"

"Relax. I'm not questioning your word - or at least your comprehension of your word." Jake pretended to look around more closely at the paintings covering the walls of the gallery as he moved, apparently randomly, toward the wall near the door, assuming enough time had elapsed for the next part of the plan. "Not your word, Wilson - but just as with the selection of items you have stolen for your collection - I'm really only questioning your judgment." To accent the word "judgment" Jake turned to face Wilson directly and used his elbow to smash the fire alarm box on the wall now directly behind him.

Chapter 32

Jake waiting, poised to move for the door, as a piercing wail cut off any further comments. Wilson, however, did not flinch, but rather shook his head and pulled a white cell phone from his front left pocket - tapping a few numbers. "What did you think that would accomplish?" he shouted to be heard above the noise. "It doesn't connect to the authorities in any way. It is an alarm for me only."

The sound ended suddenly, washing the room in silence as Wilson put the phone back into his pocket. He added, now quietly, "And I assure you, no one will hear it outside of this house." Standing between Jake and the door, he slowly reached into the back pocket of his pants and removed a small gun. "I see that not only have I underestimated your talents, I have overestimated your good sense. Your careless move just now has made me realize that I need to dispose of you right away."

In the moments of alarm, while Wilson punched the code on his cell phone, Jake moved to the left, now standing directly in front of the Just Judges panel. As Wilson gave a slight jiggle to the gun in his hand, Jake leaned to one side. "Careful now. Don't be too quick to fire that thing. There's a lot of value on these walls, and small handguns can be difficult to aim properly." As Wilson paused, looking at the best pieces of his collection, Jake moved further to the left, staying out of Wilson's direct reach. "You can damage anything in this room, and at the same time kill the only person you have under your control who can fix it."

Wilson said nothing, apparently unsure of what to do next. "So let's just take a breath and figure out how to get out of this. Both of us," Jake said, continuing to circle the room. "You with your Eve panel and me with my life."

"There's no way out for you. You know that."

As Wilson responded, Jake removed a small lighter from his pocket. "Butane. Not much of a weapon against a person, I admit. But against a work of art?" He held the lighter to his right, now directly in front of a painting by Titian. "Not much of a weapon. Two Euros at the Pharmacie - but enough, wouldn't you say?"

Wilson did not move. "Do you think I'm stupid? I know that you would be shot and killed before you could set fire to anything with that little pocket lighter."

"True," Jake said, as he pushed his thumb and broke the top off the plastic lighter. "However, Butane is an alkane. Have you ever seen the damage caused to an oil painting from even the slightest splash of any alkane? I have, and it's devastating." Jake didn't move, hoping Wilson's chemical knowledge was as flimsy as most people's.

Wilson did not move.

"What if I did help you switch and steal the Eve panel? What if I was at the center of both the theft and the forgery? That would put me as deeply into the shit as you. Right? Your capture would guarantee my capture, and vice-versa. Right?" Wilson took a step closer and Jake held the lighter directly over the Titian, tilting it slightly to the side. "Back off and think. Am I right?"

Wilson's expression changed to a half-smile as he stepped back. "Perhaps." Wilson shrugged. "And yet, here we are. How do we step back from this cliff?"

At that moment, a commotion from outside the gallery room erupted, including two shots. Wilson's face turned quickly to the door and then back to Jake, who raised his arms and shrugged. Taking advantage of the distraction, Jake turned and ran for the door. Wilson, despite his size, arrived first, locked the door and turned himself to Jake, lunging against him and dropping him to the floor.

Finding himself pinned by Wilson's massive bulk, Jake tried to move to a more advantageous position but failed, and Wilson quickly retrieved his handgun. With a grunting heave, Jake freed one arm and held Wilson's gun arm – pushing the muzzle back and forth from his face. His other arm still pinned, however, he felt himself losing the grip that prevented his execution. Wilson yanked and pulled himself free. "I thought you were smarter than this."

A single shot was followed by a crackling of wood, and Wilson turned to look back at the shattered door behind him.

"Arrêt, Wilson," Jean shouted. "Arrêt!"

Wilson seemed transfixed as first Jean and then Luc stepped into the room, guns out and pointed. His mouth open, he slowly raised his hands, reluctantly, handgun still in his grasp, to the level of his shoulders. Luc stepped forward and reached for the handgun. When he resisted, Luc cracked the muzzle of own gun against Wilson's head, which immediately began to bleed despite Wilson's complete silence during the assault. Luc pulled the gun from Wilson's grip and motioned him to get off of Jake. As Wilson's gaze turned again to Jake, a primal hatred burned behind his eyes. Slowly, his upper lip quivering in a sneer, he rose and stood.

Jean stepped forward, gun also leveled at Wilson, "The chair. Sit."

Wilson obeyed, and Jean pulled out a pair of handcuffs. With Luc on guard, Jean bent to clip Wilson's leg to the leg of the chair. His ankle, however, was too large and Jean pulled a plastic clip-strip from his pocket, neatly securing both of Wilson's legs to both of the chair legs. He stepped back as Wilson's eyes moved from Jake and now darted quickly from side-to-side.

Once secured to the chair, everything seemed to go quiet. Luc and Jean scanned the room, mouths open. Jean was shaking his head slowly in disbelief.

"A bit later than I had hoped, but well-timed, I've got to admit," Jake said. Turning to Wilson, he added, "And for the record, Butane converts to a gas almost immediately upon exposure to the air. Does buy a bit of time, however."

Luc replied, still looking at the art surrounding him. "It all went well. Your instructions from the tablet back at the studio, and Jean keyed in on the GPS chip in your shoe very easily. Yes. Went well." Luc walked to one wall for a better look. "Yes, went very well. Are these the real things? The, um—" he waved his arm searching for the word "—the real deal?"

"I'm guessing so, but we'll have to check everything."

"Yes," Jean added. "Best not to alert a museum that they own a fake unless we are sure they do. The Bureau can do all of that."

"Bureau isn't doing anything," a voice said from the door behind them. As Jake turned, he noticed the smile that had returned to Wilson's face. In the doorway, Wilson's assistant stood with another man. They stepped into the room, weapons drawn. There was a moment of silent standoff, until the assistant said over his shoulder, "The woman." He half turned to Jake and smiled. "Bring her in."

Jake's heart skipped as he saw a third man enter, holding Lily in front of him. Her hands were cuffed behind her back and her mouth was taped. The third man held a gun to her head.

"Lily!" Jean said, "What are you—"

The third man ripped the tape from Lily's mouth and, squirming in the handcuffs, she spat blood onto the floor. Lily then turned to face the others. "I messed up, Jean. I followed you. But there was no way I was going to sit on the sidelines. Then I was ambushed back in the first room."

"Okay then. Guns down and cut him loose," the assistant said.

Jean and Luc slowly placed their guns on the floor, and kicked them in the direction of Wilson's men. Jean then went over to Wilson, took out a small penknife and cut the plastic clip-strips. Wilson stood slowly, took the penknife from Jean, and swiped it across his face – cutting deep. "A little scar to remember this day," Wilson said, folding the penknife and tossing it to his assistant. "At least for as long as you will remember anything." He turned to Jake. "And you – you brought all of this on yourselves, just as you did all those years ago."

"Five," Jake said. "Five years."

Wilson signaled to his assistant. "Check this man's pockets. See what he may be hiding." He turned again to Jake. "A weapon, perhaps? A transmitter? And of course remove his shoes." He laughed once in a quiet snort and turned to look at Luc. "Ah, Luc. Such talent. Such a waste."

"Collector," the assistant said, "He's clear. Nothing in his pockets. No phone, no weapon. Just this." He handed a yellow plastic prescription bottle to Wilson.

"Oxaydo?" he said, reading the label. He squinted to read the small print. "That's oxycontin, isn't it? Now why would you have something like this?"

"They're yours, actually," Jake said.

"They most certainly are not."

"It's because of the work of your assholes on my hand that I take these." Jake looked directly at Wilson. "So yes, they're yours."

Wilson looked again at the container, and nodded to himself. "So because of me you take these. Okay then, take them you shall. This bottle seems almost full. Yes, time to take your pills, Mr. Daniels. All of them." He turned to his men. "One of you get him a bottle of water."

One man turned, stepped out, and returned almost instantly, handing a small plastic bottle to Jake.

"So shall I have my men force the pills down your throat, or do you have what it takes to comply on your own?" Either way, you are a dead man - but you knew that much some time ago, apparently. At any rate, this should be an easier exit that what I have planned for your co-conspirators here." Wilson's halting speaking tone had returned with his confidence, as he glanced briefly at Luc and Jean and reached down to straighten the crease of his slacks.

"You can't!" Lily screamed. "That will kill him!"

"Well I should hope so," Wilson said. Jake grabbed the water with a swipe and took the pills from Wilson.

"I suspected as much, Mr. Daniels. This should be entertaining."

Jake swallowed half of the pills, drank from the bottle, swallowed the other half, and drank again.

There was silence in the room as Wilson looked at Jake, smiling.

Jake's head was lowering, although he fought to keep alert. Within a minute, he stumbled, caught himself, stumbled again and fell to the floor – lying on his side and moving spasmodically. He opened his mouth to speak, but only mumbled a few incoherent and rattling sounds.

Wilson turned away and looked at his assistant. "Check on him in about five minutes. If he's dead, get him out of here. And if he isn't," Wilson snorted, "Finish it. We have some cleaning up to do." He turned again to face Luc and Jean. "You could have left well-enough alone, you know. All this death here today – it is on your conscience. All of it. On you."

At which point Lily ducked under the arm holding her and head-butted the man's gun onto the floor. Her movements flashed like lightning as she turned and kicked his feet out from under him, and when he toppled, kicked his head so hard the crack echoed from the gallery walls.

Luc and Jean each went for one of the others. Luc jumped sideways to avoid the man's first wild shot, and then grabbed his gun arm and pulled him to the floor. Jean charged forward and tackled the remaining guard, and they, too, were quickly rolling on the floor. Somewhere in the room a gun reported, but the wrestling continued. Wilson's eyes went wide as he reacted to each gunshot by looking around the walls of his gallery. He then bent to retrieve one of the guns still lying on the floor where it had been kicked earlier.

An oak panel – especially one that is 600 years old – can be a brittle thing, and smashing someone over the head with such a weapon would shatter it and do little more than annoy the intended target. However, an oak panel – even one that it 600 years old – when swung from the side, as a scythe, displays incredible lateral force. So when Jake rose to his knees, grabbed the portion of the Eve panel that he had brought from the studio, and slammed it sideways into Wilson's knee, the tendons surrounding the patella, and connecting the Femur to the Fibula, exploded, dropping Wilson to the ground. And when the guard who had been wrestling with Jean scrambled over to help his boss, Jake slammed the panel sideways into his skull – with much the same effect.

Suddenly, the room was still, the only sounds coming from the massive prostrate form of Wilson, and the squirming form of Jean, grabbing at his abdomen. Dark blood was oozing between his fingers.

Lily, petite and athletic, had managed to squat and pull her cuffed hands down around her bottom and over her legs. She was next to Jean, crying both with fear and with anger. "Luc, call the Bureau, and tell them an agent is down. We need an ambulance now. Also an overdose kit. We have to get help to Jake before it's too late." Only a moment later did she realize that Jake was standing. "Jake?"

"No need for the overdose kit, Luc," Jake said. "Just the ambulance. Fortunately these guys didn't understand how long before oxy takes effect."

"True, but we still will need that kit, even if it isn't for another hour or so."

Jake shook his head. "No, we won't." He looked over at the shocked expression on Lily's face. "After I kicked the habit, I had to find a way to fight the temptation to go back on the oxy. So I filled a bottle with fakes. I kept them close to me or in my pocket all the time to remind me – part of my therapy, I guess you'd say. Still, they aren't real. Just sugar and flour."

He walked over to Jean and Lily. "How bad is it the wound?"

There was a gunshot, and Lily and Jake both jumped and turned. Luc was standing over the body of Wilson, smoke still rising from the gun's muzzle. He turned to them. "Had to do it. He was going for the gun on the floor."

There was a long pause. Jake finally said, "Luc, you are already under investigation. You can't be holding that when the authorities arrive. Give me the gun, let it be my prints on it. I don't have a record with these police or with the FBI. When I tell them it was self-defense, they'll believe me. You aren't going to be that lucky."

"Not a chance. Five years ago you took the heat for me. I think it's time I stood up for myself."

Jake looked closely at him. "Come on, Luc, this is different. Very different. Give me the gun and let me handle this."

"Yes, yes, this is different." Luc paused and turned to face Jake. "I'm truly sorry, but I have not been honest with you." He pointed the gun at Jake. "I have to ask you to sit in the chair now, while we figure out how to clean this mess."

Jake didn't move, then exhaled and shook his head. "I was hoping my suspicions were wrong about you, even when I knew better. And what do you mean 'we'?"

Two more men entered the room, guns drawn. Jake recognized them as the two guards outside Wilson's studio in Romigny. The guard Jake shot in the foot was one of them, his foot now encased in a large black boot. He glared at Jake, and his fists clenched.

Luc waved his gun toward the chair and Jake moved slowly to sit. "So that's how you managed to distract them when Lily and I drove off. A little help on the inside."

Luc nodded to the handcuffs that Jean had attempted to use on Wilson and the guard in the boot retrieved them and clamped them on Jake's wrist - as tightly as he was able - and cuffed him to the chair. Jake sat motionless and stone-faced.

"Wilson did not treat his men very well," Luc said. "I will be much more rewarding in that regard."

"So this collection becomes yours now?"

"I am the logical heir, don't you think?"

"How long have you been planning this coup? Was it part of the plan when you came to my houseboat last week?"

There was a long pause, as Luc rifled the pockets of the man who had brought Lily into the room. "Voila!" he said, holding the small key to the handcuffs. He unlocked them and Lily bent over to help her husband.

"Lily," Jake said from the chair. "That piece we both felt we were missing? Here it is," he nodded his head toward Luc. "And how bad is Jean, because I don't think the FBI is on its way." He turned to Luc. "Did you even call an ambulance?"

Luc's head moved from side to side. "I don't think Lily will be of much help to you." There was a silence as Lily moved to help her husband, ignoring Luc's comment. Jake scanned the scene – Lily and Jean, Luc, the two guards, the bodies on the floor, the masterpieces on the walls surrounding them – but said nothing. "I never wanted it to go this way," Luc said quietly. "Neither did Lily, I'm quite sure. Believe me, please."

"So when did you change your mind and decide that you could arrange to 'inherit' all of this? Was it back in Baltimore? Before that? It was a pretty sloppy plan, so I'm guessing it changed somewhere along the way."

Luc looked over at Jake. "I had been working for some time to take over from Wilson. He was not in the best of health, as you can no doubt deduce. But understand, when I brought the Pissarro to you, it was honestly for you to hide until I could turn it over to the authorities in Washington. It was to be a revelation - a good will gift – mitigating the heart of the investigation against me, and really just a minor loss to this collection. Then when the gunman tried to kill me, I realized that to be the – what is the word – whistleblower - would only mean that one day Wilson would send someone else who would be successful and I would be dead."

"So you decided to change plans and switch Pissarros?"

Luc raised his head and looked at Jake. "What are you talking about?"

Jake leaned back reflexively and looked away in thought. After a moment, he nodded to himself. "Well shit, then."

As he turned to look again at Jean and Lily, he noticed that she was weeping, her head turned away.

"No." Jean raised his head and struggled to lift himself to one elbow. "I did that. I switched the painting."

Jake waited a beat. "But that's not possible, is it Lily?"

"So," Luc said, "the Pissarro is gone?" He chuckled and shook his head. "Such irony. It is almost Shakespearean."

"Lily," Jake said, his voice quieter. "What have you done?"

She raised her chin. "Only what I had to do. Just that."

"But you are going to need to call the Bureau. You know that, right?"

Lily said nothing.

"I know that the Bureau is investigating you," Jake added.

Lily's eyebrows raised in surprise, and then lowered with her realization. "Of course they are."

"I've been in touch with the detective in Baltimore who was investigating Luc's apparent death."

"Martik?"

"Um-hm. And he has been informed of the investigation into your actions – although he didn't know any specifics. He also informed me of the switch of Pissarros at the boat. I have to admit, I was pretty dense about the whole thing, but the pieces finally fell into place. Nobody other than Luc or you could have switched that painting. And when Jean tried to confess just now, you weren't shocked, surprised, horrified – nothing at all."

"Where is the Pissarro?" Luc said, interrupting the silence.

"Shut up," Jake said, addressing Luc but not taking his eyes off Lily. "This is more than your damned stolen Pissarro. You want to fuck up your own life, that's one thing – but this?" Jake turned to look directly at Luc. "I believed in you! Even when I knew someone else was lying on that slab in Baltimore I held my belief that you had good reason and needed help. I killed a man because of you!" he said. He then looked at the man with the smashed head on the floor. "Two men, in fact." He turned again to look at Luc, shaking his head. "I can no longer look at myself and see a man of peace and honor, Luc. That's because, despite my common sense, I tried to believe in you. And so did Lily. And what has that done for her?"

Lily stepped closer to the two men. "The Pissarro is already in the hands of the D'Orsay. They received it through a third party yesterday, with just enough explanation to keep all of us out of the spotlight. How they handle it is up to them."

Jake turned to Lily. "So what is it you are doing? Why are you under investigation?" Unable to hide the anger in his voice, he added. "Tell me now before 'my friend' here shoots me."

"Jake," Luc added, although his voice echoed from the background, "I don't want to do that."

Lily sighed heavily. "I knew what Jean was doing – and I knew why, although he never told me outright.

There is no money in what we do, Jean and I. We work for the Bureau for – what – twenty years? Then what? A minimal pension to follow years of minimal salary?" Lily paused and extended her hands. "But that's okay for me. I knew the sacrifices before going with the Bureau, and I didn't care. We get by. But Jean couldn't feel that way, he couldn't accept it. So he hooked up with Luc here to cash in."

"Exactly!" Luc said, suddenly. "This is a victimless crime! And even now there is more than enough here." He looked back and forth from Jake to Lily. "More than enough for all of us to be wealthy for the rest of our days. Even just the reward money for some of these. Stolen paintings are returned. We are heroes, aren't we?" He looked again at Jake and Lily, both of whom remained silent. "And then the pieces which actually belonged to Wilson, they could be auctioned at unbelievable amounts. That's good all around, isn't it?"

There was silence in the gallery, broken only by the heavy breathing of Jean and the squeak of the boot of the man Jake shot. "No," Jake said, shaking his head. "Not good. Not good at all."

"Lily? You understand." Luc said.

Lily lowered her head. "No Luc. It's over, and I'm glad it's over." She turned again to Jake. "I knew what Jean was doing, but I didn't want to confront him. He saved my life, Jake!" Sobbing, she continued. "So I followed his trail, cleaning up after him. They were only minor indiscretions, at first. Then there were falsified reports. It got worse up until the stealing of the Pissarro. I tried to undo what he was doing, without him ever knowing it."

"And in doing so," Jake added. "You became the focus of an investigation."

Lily nodded and pulled a phone from her pocket. "But I didn't know about the Pissarro when I saw you in Baltimore. I realized the truth that evening in your condo." Lily shook her head, deciding something final to herself. "Time to end this. I'm calling the Bureau."

"Put the phone away! You're not calling anyone!" Luc said, a tremor in his voice.

"Or what, Luc? Are you going to kill me too? Kill us all? I've already made a first contact."

Luc was breathing heavily – looking from Jake to Lily and back to Jake. "You are giving me no choice! Why are you making me do this?" he said, his voice cracking.

"We aren't making you do anything, Luc," Jake said.

And then they all heard a click. Actually, they heard three clicks.

"Nobody moves!" a voice announced, echoed by another voice, "Personne ne bouge!"

Luc, Lily and Jake turned as one to see three men – and three rifles. Two of the rifles were pointed at the two guards who had come to Luc's assistance. The man who spoke first had his rifle pointed directly at Luc.

"I want all weapons on the floor, kicked this way, then everyone on the floor – face down. Is that clear to everyone?" The two guards and Luc slowly complied.

Jake sat handcuffed to his chair, and Lily stood preparing to remove her FBI credentials. "You also, agent Nicole. On the floor."

While one of the two men walked around and clip-stripped the wrists of Luc, Luc's two guards, and Lily, the other stepped over to examine Jean, nodding that he appeared to be in no immediate danger.

The first man spoke. "You must be Jacob Daniels then."

Jake nodded from the chair. "And you are--?"

"Thomas Fallsborough, FBI by way of Interpol, currently on loan to the French Legat." He motioned to Luc. "Key, Mr. Benoit. Where?"

Luc moved his hand to the back pocket of his pants and Fallsborough pushed it away, retrieving the small handcuff key himself. "Now what brings you to this party?" Luc said, his voice muffled.

Fallsborough looked down at Luc's prostrate form. "Interesting question. I am actually seeking Ms. Nicole over there, and was given a tip through the FBI's attaché from which we were able to find you all here. Finding you, Mr. Benoit, is merely a fortunate coincidence." He turned to Jake. "So we can begin by you telling me what it going on here, Mr. Daniels."

Jake tilted his head. "Can you undo these cuffs first?"

Fallsborough walked over and released Jake from the handcuffs. "Of course, my apologies." He stepped back. "And by the way, were you the source of that tip?"

Jake shook his head and heard Lily speak, still face-down on the floor. "That was me, agent."

All eyes briefly turned to Lily, who moved her head to the side. "Turning myself in, I suppose."

Fallsborough turned to one of the two agents. "Agent Starson, let's get that man some medical attention, while we sort this whole thing out. Agent Marion, stick around. I think I'm going to need a second note taker – and witness. Mr. Daniels, it's time to talk."

Chapter 33

Harris and Mele listened as the police siren became louder and then stopped. They heard the light clack of shoes running up the marble steps, pause at the shattered door handle, then step quickly into the room. Martik stood, service revolver drawn, mouth open slightly as he scanned the room and took in the scene.

"Thank you for coming so quickly, detective," Mele said. "We've tried not to touch anything, as I'm sure you would like to examine the—" she gave a small wave of her arm around the room, "—the scene."

"I, umm, are you both all right?" Martik said, still looking around the room. "Is anyone hurt?"

"You mean other than these two," Harris pointed to the two bodies on the floor. "No, Mele and I are okay." He turned to his wife. "Wouldn't you agree, love?"

Mele nodded. "I am sorry to say that I took that man's knife," she pointed to the body prone and unmoving at Martik's feet. "I put it on the coffee table, to keep it out of the way of things. I hope that doesn't corrupt anything."

"Oh," Harris added, "Also, Mele brought me two dish cloths. We figured that, as long as I was standing on this man's arms, I might as well use the cloths to stop the bleeding."

Martik nodded reflexively, placing his gun back into the holster under his jacket. He bent to the man at his feet and felt at the neck for a pulse. "So... I'm guessing they broke in the door..."

"Yes," Harris said. "They wanted the painting, so they must have had some reason for not believing your false public notice. This man," he pointed to the body beneath him, "had a gun. Then, just after she called you, Mele came in and threw hot coffee in their faces, and--"

"She what?"

"Threw hot coffee in their faces, and Bromo took it from there." At the sound of his name, the dog looked up and turned to see Martik, his tail suddenly wagging. "Good boy, Bromo, but stay right there." The dog returned his gaze to the face of the man on the floor, and growled quietly. The man moaned, his eyes closed.

"And this guy?" Martik said, still crouched over the first body.

"Well," Mele began "he was about to stab Harris, so I hit him with a bronze sculpture. A Rodin casting, actually. I'm afraid I must have killed him because I hit him pretty hard. But I didn't feel I had much choice."

Martik exhaled a single laugh and shook his head. "I'm sure you didn't, Mrs. Daniels. And don't worry, he isn't dead – probably has a pretty massive concussion, however. And an ambulance is on its way." He stood. "I'm guessing these two had no idea what they were getting into." He stood and looked around once more, still shaking his head. "And you are both okay? You're sure?"

Harris and Mele nodded in unison as a man in blue scrubs stepped up to the door, signaling a partner, who also entered.

"Two." Martik said. "One head trauma, one—" he looked over at the other man just as Harris was carefully stepping off his arms. "—lacerations and, um, dog trauma?"

"Bromo has had his rabies shot, however," Mele added. "All of his inoculations, in fact."

Martik smiled. "Don't worry, Mrs. Daniels. Bromo is not in any trouble here." He turned to the EMTs. "And make sure both are cuffed. They are to be regarded with criminal protocols."

The two men nodded and went to work.

"Okay, Bromo," Harris said. "Good boy." The dog stepped around the man and went over to Mele, sniffing her. He then sat at her feet, on guard and at attention.

Chapter 34:
Three months later

The occasional chill of late October in Baltimore never failed to refresh Jake, who stretched his shoulders and back before leaning into the sandpaper he had curled around a spindle on the deck of his houseboat. A few feet to his left, Martik pulled down on another wrap of sandpaper curled around a different spindle. 12 spindles lined the rail of each side of the houseboat deck, and every one needed to be sanded clean of several layers of chipped paint. Martik paused and looked up at the cypress trees along the water line. "I have to confess, Jake, this is not a bad way to spend a Sunday."

Jake smiled as the tablet moved to another song in the playlist.

"Another Dave Van Ronk?" Martik said with a grin. "Wasn't one enough?"

"It's an acquired taste," Jake said. "I'll give you that."

Martik shrugged and returned to his task as the gravelly voice began to croak out *Dink's Blues*. "Have I told you how incredible—"

"—my parents are? Only every one of the last six Sundays. But that's okay – you'll get no argument from me."

The two men worked in comfortable silence. "So what's the latest with Luc?" Jake said, setting down his sandpaper and picking up a cleaning rag.

Martik continued working. "Not completely sure. Between the French National Police, the FBI and Interpol, he's got his hands full, I'm sure. To be honest, I'm glad to be out of it. Too much to do here in Charm City as it is."

Jake nodded. "You're right. Not your mess. Nor mine, either."

Bromo, who had been sleeping on the deck between the two men, raised his head and sniffed the air. He pulled himself to his feet and sniffed the air again – looking around.

"Permission to come aboard?"

The familiar voice prompted Jake to stand and turn, and Bromo to trot to the gangplank. "Lily?"

She stood in a light blue hooded Hopkins sweatshirt and jeans, and Jake felt a piece of himself beginning to crumble. "Bromo! You sweet boy," she said, rubbing the dog behind his ears. "Detective Martik? I didn't recognize you in work clothes. I've never seen you without a suit and tie! Surprised to see you here."

Martik smiled. "I probably wouldn't have recognized myself, either. Truth is, I had to dig pretty far down to find these work clothes. But Jake convinced me to stop by, I'm guessing almost two months ago, and now I come here pretty regularly on Sundays. Let off the steam of the workweek, and enjoy a bit of physical labor along the river." He stood and dusted himself off. "Kind of a Zen thing, I think." There was a pause as Lily and Jake looked at each other. Martik wiped his hands on a clean rag. "Hey, why don't I drive up to Zaroffs and get a us some lunch?. He looked at Lily and back at Jake. "Powerhouse sandwiches all around?"

"Sounds good," Jake said.

Lily smiled and nodded. "Thanks." She then and looked around at the houseboat. "You have certainly made some progress. This is beginning to look admirable." She paused and squinted. "What is that sound?"

"Dave Van Ronk. An acquired – ah, forget it." He clicked off the tablet.

They stood, unmoving, looking at each other.

"How have you been, Jake?"

"Good." He paused. "No, really. I have been good. Much better, actually. How about you?"

She offered a half-smile. "Okay. Still processing everything."

"And Jean?"

"Can I sit?" Jake nodded and pulled a deck chair over for her. As she sat, he pulled up a box and sat on that, next to her.

Lily looked down. "Jean. Yes. Well. Jean is recovering. Out of the hospital, but still pretty restricted. Wearing an ankle band until they figure out what to do with him."

"How does it look?"

"He has a good attorney, and is playing all the legal angles to delay charges. The FBI wants nothing to do with him, of course."

"And do you?"

Lily looked up and smiled. "That's pretty blunt. But fair. And I'm not sure. Jean did what he did for us – I do believe that. And he is my husband. But I don't know how much I can overlook. Or forgive."

"Do you still love him? Jake's mouth went suddenly dry and the question came out in a hoarse whisper.

Lily paused and looked directly at him. Jake felt his chest tighten. Then she looked down. "But that's not the right question, is it? The right question is – is loving Jean enough, knowing what he was willing to do – despite his motives?" There was a long silence. "And I just don't know."

There was another long silence, as Lily looked around the boat. Jake finally said, "So why are you here? Why aren't you in Paris? Did the FBI get rid of you too?

Lily smiled. "I think they would like to, but it turns out there is more to the case – Wilson's collection, I mean -- and they still think I'm useful. I'm still working, pending reprimand."

"More to the case?"

"Yes. It seems Wilson had colleagues in the art collection/forgery/art theft game – or whatever this obsession is. They've found some of his papers that suggest other collectors. Remember that list of numbers we found in Luc's apartment? That was some sort of code he used to ID the other 'collectors.' Luc is playing that pretty coy, as you can imagine, to see what he can get out of it. Also, the provenance of

Wilson's collection is highly suspect. Returning stolen works is not as simple as you might think."

"I know. I've had some experience with that before – on a much smaller scale, of course. How are the museums taking it?"

"The Louvre is downplaying everything. The D'Orsay is going to replace the Pissarro and aren't sure whether to say anything to the public or not. You know that whole traditional museum thing..."

"I figured that. If they make too much of the story, it will just point out that they could have one of their works forged without even knowing it. Not good for the reputation – and I can see their point. And what about Ghent?"

Lily smiled. "Just the opposite. The city museum is planning a major celebration. They've created a documentary on the whole theft and forgery scandal and will play it with a grand re-unification of Van Eyck's altarpiece. Scheduling it for next year. Should be headlines world-wide. The exhibit in Brussels has been postponed until the following year – and they're fine with that because their exhibit will be all that much more spectacular."

Jake nodded. "I know, I was contacted to work with them on that documentary, but I declined. I have been trying not to follow it, in fact."

"I can see that."

"So why, then?"

"Why what?"

"Why are you here?"

Lily stood and walked across the deck to the cabin. She stepped inside and stopped at Jake's painting – still behind glass on a renovated wall of dark mahogany with brass trim. She pulled the cuff of her sweatshirt over her hand and rubbed a bit of dirt off the glass and stepped back. "I don't know. I guess I wanted to see how the boat was looking. How the renovation was going. Whether the damage of the years was irreversible, or only needed some time and some work. I wanted to see how much of the wonder and grandeur had been uncovered and revealed."

Jake stepped over next to her. "I know what you mean. And I think I can make something `of this."

Lily continued to look at the painting, smiled, and said quietly, "I'm sure you can."

CPSIA information can be obtained
at www.ICGtesting.com
Printed in the USA
LVHW080735010222
709865LV00014B/1172

9 781647 199333